SUDDENLY BARONESS

DAISY EMORY

TURBO KITTEN

Turbo Kitten Industries, PO Box 5012, Galt, CA 95632

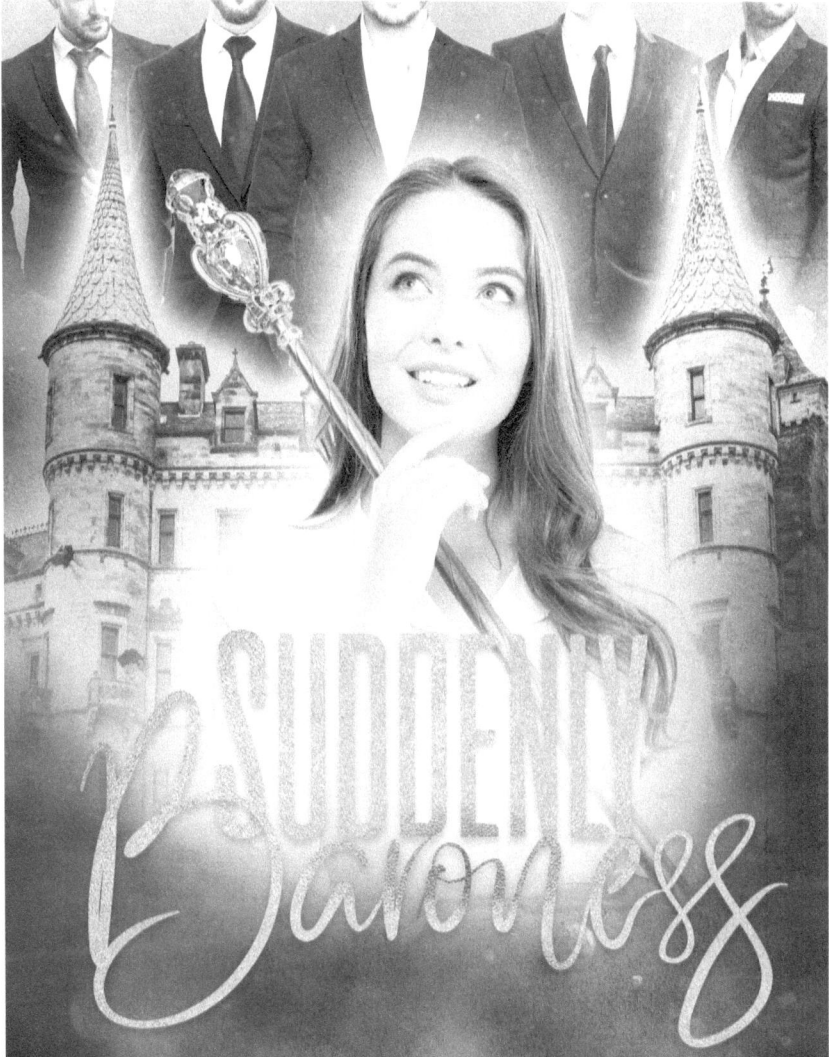

SUDDENLY
Baroness

USA TODAY BESTSELLING AUTHOR *CATHERINE BANKS*
WRITING AS

DAISY EMORY

This is dedicated to Lorie for being an amazing supporter and putting up with my rush requests.

Thank you, Avery, for being my biggest supporter, my best friend, and husband. I love you.

CHAPTER ONE

"You have three seconds to leave, or I'll blow your head off your shoulders," Shea threatened the man standing beside me.

I sighed and dropped my chin down. The evening had started off well. Shea had taken me on a date to a movie I'd been wanting to see, then out to dinner, and finally out for drinks.

We'd been in the bar for less than five minutes when a man walked up and started hitting on me while Shea was in the restroom.

Shea towered over the smaller man, his massive frame blocking the light behind him. It was easy to see how he got his mafia nickname, Ox.

Surprisingly, the man didn't cower. He was average height, handsome to the point of almost beautiful, with high cheekbones and a perfectly symmetrical face. Combined with piercing green eyes and tousle-styled dirty blonde hair, he was gorgeous. "Easy, man. I didn't know she was here with someone since she was at the bar by herself." He looked at me and smirked. "Seems I upset your bodyguard. Sorry for the inconvenience."

"Have a good night," I said with a return smile.

Shea stepped forward, bumping his shoulder against the man's as he took the spot at my side.

Once the guy was gone, I looked up at Shea with an arched brow. "What was that about, Ox?"

He flagged down the bartender, who immediately ran over to us. "Martini, dirty," he ordered.

"Margarita, no salt," I added.

"Right away," the bartender said, and got to work making the drinks.

This bar was in the Moriarty Mafia's territory. The staff was comprised of former mafia members - those who had been injured or who no longer wanted to be part of the dangerous side of the life. It was sort of a mafia semi-retirement for those who still wanted to work. Several businesses in Stephan Moriarty's territory provided similar opportunities. Stephan tried his hardest to take care of his people, even after they'd left. I thought it might also be to keep tabs on them and ensure they didn't go to another mafia and give away secrets, but I never said that thought out loud.

The one great thing about visiting places like this was that they knew who Ox was and tripped over themselves to keep him happy.

They were starting to learn who I was, and I didn't really like how they treated me. It was nice to get my drinks quickly, but it felt weird to be feared. I wasn't opposed to having certain people afraid of me, but not random people who would have been nice to me even if I wasn't part of the mafia.

"Seeing another man near you sets off my protectiveness,"

Shea answered finally. "I'm always terrified that you'll get kidnapped or hurt."

"I'm carrying," I reminded him. Even when I went out with them, they made me wear my knives and a gun. It was a tiny thing that I kept on my ankle, but it made them feel better. And while I would never admit it to them, it made me feel better, too. I was not going to get kidnapped ever again.

"I know," he whispered as he set his hand against my cheek. His palm was bigger than my face, and he basically cupped my entire head in it. "You're the most important thing in the world to me, Amelia. I would tear apart the world to find you."

Smiling wide, I jumped up to reach his lips for a quick press of my lips against his. "I love you, too, Oxie Loxie."

"Your drinks," the bartender said as he set them down on the bar before us and then scurried away.

Shea slipped his arm around my waist as we turned back to the bar to get our drinks. "So, how anxious are you to get home?" he asked.

I cringed. "Is it that obvious?"

He laughed softly. "Yeah."

"Sorry," I said as I sipped my drink. "It's just the first time I've been away from the babies for this long." My twins were only six months old, and I hadn't been away from them for more than an hour. This was the longest I'd gone without holding them, and I was having withdrawals already.

"I know, and I'm glad that I was the lucky one to get you out of the house for this long," he said, bending to kiss the top of my head.

The men in my life were swoon-worthy and liked to say the sweetest things. It was like they wanted me to be jelly in their arms all the time. Sometimes I wondered if they prac-

ticed their lines with each other or had an idea board somewhere they wrote suggestions to use.

Suddenly, the front door burst open as a deep male voice
yelled, "Everyone on the floor," and two gunshots fired.

Shea and I dropped down into a squat, grabbed our guns,
and looked to see what was going on. Shea was blocking me,
and I had to lean pretty far to see around him.

At the door stood three masked men, each carrying a
shotgun.

"Let's make this easy. We're going to pass around a bag,
and you're going to put your valuables inside it," the one in
the middle said.

"Ox?" I asked softly, waiting for his decision on what to do.
We could shoot them or play along until they left and then
follow them to teach them a lesson or call for reinforcements.

"Call," he whispered back after a second of hesitation.

Hiding behind his bulk, I pulled my cell phone out and hit
the emergency call button. It was programmed to group call
all of the guys at once.

"Tiger's Bar. Armed robbery," I said when I heard at least
one of them answer.

"On our way," Arcadio said immediately.

"Tell Shea not to engage unless your life is in danger,"
Stephan ordered.

"Yes, sir," Shea replied.

"Hey! Who's on their phone? Who the fuck is on their
phone?" the robber on the right demanded.

I quickly hung up and pocketed my phone. "Your bulk
really does come in handy."

Shea snickered. "That's what she said."

I rolled my eyes even though he couldn't see it.

"Guns away," he whispered.

"Already put mine back," I replied.

He slipped his gun into his jacket, and one of the robbers noticed.

"Oy! Hands where I can see them!" he shouted and aimed the gun at Shea.

Shea pulled out his wallet and held his hands up. "Just getting my wallet like you ordered us."

"You just keep your hands up, big man," the guy said, and I could hear a slight quiver in his voice that betrayed his fear.

Yeah, I'd be pretty scared if I saw Shea with his hand in his jacket, too.

"Hurry up!" the robber with the bag yelled at a petite woman, who shook wildly as she tried to unclip her necklace.

"You're a damn danger magnet," Shea muttered. "I've been to this bar thousands of times, yet the first time I bring you here, a robbery happens. Who the fuck robs a bar?"

The door to the bar opened with a bang as Arcadio, Dane, and Forrest stormed inside, weapons aimed at the three robbers. All three had digitized masks on. As part of a strategy to hide our identities Stephan spread bunch of rumors about a war between himself and the "Moriarty Mafia", and insisted they start wearing the masks to hide our dual lives. The masks had digital screens so we could change what was on them as we pleased. Arcadio's had red, diamond-shaped eyes with a red-stitched mouth. Dane's had blue X-shaped eyes and blue fangs. Forrest's had no eyes and a green mouth full of sharp teeth.

How the hell had they gotten here so quickly? Were they waiting nearby?

I wouldn't put it past them. They were incredibly protective of me … not that I was complaining. I liked that they cared about me enough to spend the night nearby just in case I needed them.

"Whoa!" one of the robbers yelled and aimed his shotgun towards them.

"Drop your weapons now, or we kill you," Forrest instructed calmly.

"Do you know whose territory this is?" Dane asked.

"Territory? What are you talking about?" the robber on the left asked.

"Are you tourists?" I asked with a laugh and shook my head. "You've got to be from out of town."

Stephan walked in wearing his mask, and I swallowed hard at the sight of his fit frame in his suit. He'd ordered a custom mask to hide his identity, with special technology to constantly change the appearance, so he could never be identified. Unlike the others, his made you think you were looking at an actual human face. It was also bulletproof. Couldn't let the boss die, after all. It also had a voice changer to help distort and hide his voice.

He adjusted a cufflink and stood just in front of the trio. "You definitely aren't from here if you're stupid enough to try this bullshit in my territory."

"Oh, shit. It's the Moriarty Mafia," a guy near us whispered. "I'd heard a mafia family ran this area but never had confirmation."

"I heard Stephan Moriarty and the Moriarty Mafia are constantly fighting because Mr. Moriarty hates that they're using his name and making people think he might be a bad guy," the girl he was with whispered.

"Drop your weapons, and I'll let this slide," Stephan said. He looked over at me, and I grinned but hid it when the girl next to us turned to look at me.

"Who are you?" the robber nearest us asked Stephan.

"I'm the leader of the Moriarty Mafia," Stephan replied. "Not to be confused with that pansy-ass Stephan Moriarty."

"He's not a pansy!" I snapped, playing my role as Stephan's wife.

All three robbers turned towards me, their weapons coming with them and aiming in my direction.

"Drop your weapons!" Arcadio yelled and took a step forward.

Forrest chambered a round in his shotgun. "Now!"

Having dumbly given them their backs to look at me, the robbers realized they no longer had the advantage and set their guns down, and raised their arms.

Stephan walked over to me, grabbed me by the throat, and lightly squeezed. He lifted as he continued to gently press on my throat, making me stand up. "Moriarty's wife. How kind of you to grace us with your presence."

I squeezed my thighs together, turned on by this act we put on. "You may be scary, but Stephan is a better man than you'll ever be."

Stephan stepped closer to me, pinning me against the bar. "Sweetheart, you've got no idea what I'm capable of."

He'd hidden his asexuality for so long, pretending to be the ultimate playboy billionaire, that he was amazingly well-versed in flirting.

"Just let her go. You don't want to go down this path," Shea rumbled threateningly, getting into the act. Did he like getting to threaten Stephan like this? I know I would.

Stephan released me and stepped back. "You're lucky these punks were in my territory, princess. Tell your spoiled rich brat of a husband that he's welcome; I saved you, now he owes me one."

"He doesn't owe you shit," I snapped in fake outrage.

Shea placed a hand on my arm, and I clamped my lips closed.

"See you soon, princess," Stephan said cockily as he leaned in close to inhale a whiff of my perfume before he spun and sauntered out of the room.

Forrest and Dane grabbed the three guys and forced them out of the bar, dumping the few belongings they'd managed to grab on a table as they walked out.

Arcadio grabbed their discarded guns and then followed them out, saluting the bar with one of the guns. I could imagine the smile on his face as he left, even if I couldn't see it.

"Well, that was exciting," a woman beside me whispered.

I scoffed and said, "Mafia trash."

"Come on, let's go home," Shea said.

With a quick chug, I downed my drink and then nodded. "Okay."

He chuckled and downed his drink, too. "He's probably waiting."

We walked outside, turned down the nearest alleyway, and a smile lifted my lips at the sight of the SUV parked and waiting for us.

Shea had been right.

When we climbed inside, Stephan smiled at me. "Have fun?"

I leaned over and kissed him lightly on the lips. "Lots."

"I'm glad," he said.

Shea got into the driver's seat and started the SUV. "The other three handling those robbers?" Shea asked.

Stephan nodded. "Yep. They're going to drop them off at the police station with our contact."

It was nice having some of our people on the inside so we could handle situations like this easily.

"That contact likely deserves a bonus since we send a lot of things his way," I commented.

"Oh, there's a lot more than you're aware of," Stephan said. "It's best if you're in the dark about them, though."

Now my curiosity was piqued. "Rude. You know I hate not knowing things." Now that my interest was piqued, I would search our files the next time I was free and see what I could find. Hopefully, I would do it well enough that not even Forrest would know I had been snooping.

He chuckled. "So, what are you doing the rest of the night?"

"Probably going to sleep," I admitted. "After cuddling the babies, of course."

"Your mom doesn't seem to want to leave," Shea commented.

I shrugged. "She's got grandbabies she can take care of and nothing else really holding her down since Stanley and Randolph travel wherever she wants. Why would she leave?" A thought crossed my mind. "Unless she's bothering you?"

Shea shook his head. "Nope. Not at all. I just thought she would leave after a little bit to get back to her life."

"She'll leave soon, I'm sure. She can't stay anywhere for too long. That's why she owns property in multiple locations."

"Speaking of property," Stephan said. "We're going to be flying out in a few weeks. Are you prepared?"

I shook my head and sighed. "I am really not looking forward to flying so far with babies."

"It can't be helped," Shea said. "It's either we leave them here with your mom, leave you here to stay with them, or we take them."

"I don't want to be away from them," I whispered. Even though I wasn't breastfeeding either of them, I didn't like the idea of being away from my babies for more than a few hours.

Stephan reached over and patted my hand. "No one said you had to be. We're just giving you the options."

"Should I be okay with leaving them? What if something happens and we aren't here? What if they get sick?" My heart started pounding.

Stephan squeezed my hand. "It's okay, Amelia. We don't like the idea of being away from them either. It's easier to keep them safe if we are together than if we were across the world from them."

"Do we have our flights and everything planned?" I asked.

Shea nodded. "Dane already purchased all of our tickets and is finalizing the itinerary."

Getting to fly out of the country, visit a place I'd never seen before, and see one of Stephan's properties, a castle no less, was very exciting.

Yet, I was worried. I couldn't explain precisely what I was concerned about. A sense of impending doom hovered around me when I thought about our trip.

As soon as we arrived at our house, I ran into the nursery to see my babies.

Mom held up a hand from the rocking chair she sat in. The lights were dimmed, and soft music played from the speakers we'd installed after discovering they enjoyed sleeping with music on.

Currently, Johnny Cash was playing.

Dressed comfortably in footed zip-up onesies, Callen and Paige were asleep lying on their backs in their cribs. Their little mouths were open, and they looked so peaceful, like adorable little cherubs.

After a quick, silent moment to ensure they were breathing, I gave my mom a kiss on the cheek and walked out of the room again.

Shea stood in the hallway, a small smile on his face. "They good?"

I nodded. "Sleeping with Mom watching over them."

Mom stepped out of the room a moment later. "How was your date?"

"Great," I replied immediately.

"How bad was she twitching to get home?" Mom asked Shea.

He chuckled. "Not as bad as expected. I was actually pretty impressed."

Mom patted my back. "Good job, kid."

"You know you don't have to stay here, right?" I asked. "We're capable of taking care of them."

She put her hands on her hips and narrowed her eyes. "Are you trying to get rid of me?"

I held my hands up in surrender. "I would never."

Shea coughed to cover up a laugh.

"Any trouble tonight?" I asked Mom.

She shook her head. "They were perfect angels."

"Better than their mother," Shea muttered.

Mom arched a brow.

"It wasn't my fault! How can you possibly blame me for guys coming into the bar we were at to rob the people?"

"Wait, someone robbed a bar? Who the hell does that?" Mom demanded.

"That's what I asked," Shea said. "Amelia is a magnet for trouble."

"I wonder where she gets that from," Stanley, my biological

father and former mafia boss of one of the largest mafias in history, said as he rounded the corner.

Mom glared. "I don't like your insinuation one bit. I don't attract danger."

"No, you just cause it," Randolph, one of my mother's husbands, replied as he followed Stanley. Shortly after Mom reunited with Stanley, she decided she wanted to marry both Stanley and Randolph. They'd agreed and had tied the knot without even inviting me. I was only a little bitter about that.

"Maybe it's genetic," I suggested as I looked at Stanley. Stanley had been such a notorious mafia boss in his prime that he'd had to fake his own death to prevent people from coming after him. Even Mom had believed he was dead for decades.

Mom let out a bark of laughter while walking over to kiss Stanley's cheek. The two were working on repairing their relationship, and even though I could tell they loved each other and were improving, they still had a long way to go in terms of trust. Mom was still really upset that he'd let her think he was dead for so long.

Stanley wrapped her up in a hug and peppered her face with kisses. "She might be right."

"With that terrifying prophecy, I'm off to bed," Shea said. He looked down at me. "Care to join me?"

I held my arms up and said, "Carry me."

He pulled me into a bridal carry without hesitation, his strong arms holding me tightly against his chest. "As you wish."

CHAPTER TWO

"I'm pretty sure ten pairs of underwear is enough for a one-week trip," Arcadio said. He lay on my bed, shirtless, playing with one of his daggers and doing his best to distract me.

It was working.

"What if a pair breaks or gets ruined somehow? You know I'm prone to ruining clothes." Or having the clothes ruined when I got into danger. I couldn't count how many pairs of clothes I'd bled on and had to throw away. Not that I'd throw underwear away for having blood on them; that was just insanity for a woman to even consider. As old as I was, you would think I would know how to get blood out of my clothes, but I just never got the hang of it.

"We can always buy you new ones while we're there. It's another country, but they still have clothes."

"Oh, I plan on buying clothes while I'm there," I admitted. "But not to wear while I'm there."

He shook his head and chuckled. "You're so silly sometimes."

"I know I'm forgetting something," I muttered as I looked at the piles of clothes I'd laid out in preparation for packing.

Arcadio sat up, reached over, and grabbed my wrist.

I let him pull me to the bed and down on top of him. Leaning up on my elbows, I placed my hands on his chest and smiled as I gazed down at the man who'd risked his life for me and now had a permanent scar as a reminder.

He smiled and kissed my lips lightly. "Whatever you forget, we will buy you a new one when we're in Scotland. Trust me, you won't even need anything except your phone and us once we get there. You'll be too busy sightseeing and enjoying your time."

"I'm enjoying my time right now." I ran my fingertips over his chest, leaned forward, and kissed his neck.

He let out a shaky breath, slid his hands down my back to cup my butt, and pressed me against his hips as he arched them up.

I stood, pulled my shirt off with quick movements, unclasped my bra, and slid my pants down to my ankles.

Arcadio chuckled as he removed his pants and boxers at an annoyingly slow rate, although I took the opportunity to thoroughly enjoy the sight of his toned body as he stripped. My assassin was ripped, and I licked my lips to keep in the drool.

He pounced on me, kissing all over my face, neck, and down to my breasts as one of his hands slid down low, and two fingers plunged inside me.

I was already soaking wet and didn't need much work to orgasm, my muscles tightening around his fingers.

"Fuck," he breathed and sucked one of my nipples into his mouth, swirling his tongue around the taut peak and making me moan.

"Please," I begged as he made me orgasm again from his fingers.

"Please what?" he asked.

"I want you inside of me."

He didn't hesitate, removing his fingers in record time, and slid into me in just a couple of short and fast strokes.

Arcadio was one of my fast-paced lovers, preferring to make me orgasm five times in a matter of minutes and then cuddle for half an hour.

Tonight, he took his time, drawing out all of my orgasms and making me whimper whenever he changed his speed or angle to hold things up.

"Arcadio," I huffed after he stopped once.

He chuckled, kissed my lips, and slammed into me.

"Yes!" I screamed and arched up into him.

We went fast and hard until we were both coated in sweat and were left panting and satisfied on the bed.

He left me to shower while I cleaned up the room, a satisfied smile on my face.

After grabbing some snacks from the kitchen, I headed to the living room, where I could hear Arcadio playing with Callen and Paige. They loved when he played peek-a-boo with them, and I could hear their little laughs and happy coos.

Our new living room was around fifteen hundred square feet, had three leather couches, six recliners with massage and heated seats and backs, and a coffee table that was more like a low dining table due to its size. I was fairly certain it was Japanese in style, but I hadn't been the one to purchase it. There was also a lot of open rooms that I was sure would come in handy when Callen and Paige were older.

Arcadio sat cross-legged in front of the twins' swings, making faces at them. The swings had been Mom's idea, and

I'd kissed her about a dozen times for the suggestion when Callen had gotten sick a month ago and had kept me up three nights in a row. He'd had so much extra mucus that he couldn't sleep. The swings, which could be tilted, had been a lifesaver, allowing him to sleep slightly upright. The movement and sounds had kept him asleep.

They both loved the swings and often took naps in them.

I set the lemonade I'd brought on the coffee table and squatted down beside Arcadio, placing a kiss on his cheek. "Anyone do floor time with them yet?"

"Not yet," he answered.

"I'll grab their toys," Dane offered and stood from the couch where he had been reading a news article on his phone.

"Purrfect," I purred. Hitting the stop button on their swings, I waited until they came to a stop, lifted the little food tray that helped hold them in, and unbuckled them from the swing. I laid them on their backs about a foot and a half apart. "Alright, today is the day, Callen. You're going to roll over before Paige! I know you can do it. You're going to roll over and push yourself up on your arms and crawl. You can do it!"

Paige was already starting to crawl, albeit unsteadily, but Callen had so far only pushed himself up on his arms and hadn't tried to crawl. He reached for toys and would smack them on the ground, but he wouldn't crawl to retrieve toys that rolled away.

Callen smiled at me and kicked his legs.

"He'll probably be just like his mama and act like he isn't as advanced, and the next moment he's walking before all the other kids." She shook her head as she took a seat on the far couch. "You know how many doctor's appointments I took you to, afraid there was something wrong with you? Then you surpass all the other kids in the next few months. Always been a smart ass."

"I learned from the best," I said, glancing up to give her a wide smile.

Paige rolled over, drawing my attention back to them.

"Great job, Paige!" I praised.

She pushed up onto her arms and started babbling as she looked at her brother.

Callen rolled over and arched his back up before letting his head lay back down on the ground.

I cooed at them. "You can do it. You've got this, buddy."

Callen pushed up onto his elbows and babbled.

Dane set a small basket of plastic toys beside me.

I took out Callen's favorite, a clear plastic cylinder with multicolored beads inside that rattled, with some bright cog-shaped pieces on the outside he could chew on. "Come get it, Callen."

Dane took out Paige's favorite rattle and shook it. "Come on, Paige."

Paige babbled several "ah, oh, eh," sounds and slowly crawled towards Dane.

Callen turned in the direction she was headed and lowered himself back to his stomach. He used his arms to help turn his body towards her and started crawling. He wobbled much more than Paige, but the little stinker crawled faster than her and got the rattle before she could.

"I knew it!" I whispered with a wide smile. "I knew today was the day."

Once he had the rattle, I helped him into a sitting position so he could play with it easier.

"Stinker," Dane said with a proud smile. "You just wanted Mama here to see you do it, didn't you?"

Paige took the baton I offered her, and I sat her upright as well.

Both babbled as they waved, smacked, and chewed on their toys.

"So, what are your plans today?" Arcadio asked.

"She's going on a date with me," Dane answered as I opened my mouth.

I looked at him with a smirk. "I am?"

He nodded. "Yep. You let Ox take you out, so now it's my turn."

"Oy, I was just going to ask her out," Arcadio snapped.

Dane smirked and shrugged one shoulder. "You snooze; you lose."

"Fight you for it," Arcadio said with narrowed eyes.

Dane rolled his shoulders and stood. "I've been needing some exercise, and it's been a while since I've whipped your ass."

They were going to go spar for the chance to take me on a date. "I want to watch!" I yelled but looked back at the babies still playing with their toys.

"Nope, you stay here and play with Callen and Paige. We'll be right back." Dane squatted back down to kiss my cheek. "This won't take long anyway."

"I cannot wait to wipe that smug expression off your face," Arcadio said and danced from side to side on the balls of his feet.

"You know the rules," Stephan said as he entered the room, looking down at his tablet. "Clean up any blood you get on the mats. I'm tired of buying new ones because you keep forgetting to have them cleaned."

"Whoever bleeds has to clean their blood off," Arcadio said.

"Deal," Dane agreed.

Forrest walked in behind Stephan. "What's going on?"

"They're fighting for the chance to take Amelia on a date tonight," Stephan answered.

"Were you eavesdropping in the hallway?" I smirked as I asked, knowing he had probably just stopped walking right outside because something on his tablet had interested him that much.

Stephan shrugged a shoulder. "Is it eavesdropping if it's my house and my wife?"

Mom snickered as she, Randolph, and Stanley came into the room. "This is why Stephan is my favorite."

"You're not supposed to have favorites," I reminded her. Callen dropped the rattle, and I held it back out to him before he could start crying.

"I'm in for this fight," Forrest said and followed behind Dane and Arcadio. "I came here to ask her out, too."

Mom smirked. "You're so popular."

"Did your husbands fight over you, too?" I asked.

She nodded. "Happened all the time when we were younger."

"Randolph's kicked my ass enough times that I don't try anymore," Stanley said. "He's quick for his age, and I'm slow."

Mom snickered. "I told you that you need to start taking joint supplements. You're not getting any younger, Mr. Marvél."

Stanley silently mimicked her with his eyes crossed.

Mom reached over and lightly punched his arm.

Stephan set his tablet on the table and sat down on the floor beside me. He reached out, took Callen's hand, and bounced it a bit. "Look at you sitting up and playing so well."

"He crawled," I reported proudly.

Stephan's head whipped to the side to look at me, his eyes wide. "Really?"

I nodded, my smile growing. "Swear."

He snatched his tablet off the table, tapped on the screen a few times to open the security footage app, and pulled up the footage from this room to watch it. His shock turned into a huge smile as he watched it happen. He set his tablet down to pick up Callen and hug him. "I'm so proud of you, Callen."

Tears pricked my eyes as I watched him loving on Callen. I couldn't lie and say I hadn't been worried about how he would act with the kids since he knew, without a doubt, they weren't his. He had surpassed every worry I'd had as one of their fathers, though.

"Want to take them on a walk in the garden?" Stephan asked me. "The sunlight will be good for them, and it's warm enough that they won't need jackets."

I nodded emphatically. "Yes, please." I scooped up Paige, and we walked to the nursery to put pants on them since they were just in onesies currently. Once they were dressed, I asked for Stephan's tablet.

He smirked. "Want to see who's winning?"

"Don't you dare tell them," I ordered with a scowl as I accessed the security footage from the gym.

Dane was on his back on the mat, panting with a hand on his chest.

Arcadio stood beside him, smiling smugly and talking. I didn't need the audio to know he was trash talking Dane for losing.

Forrest stepped onto the mat and stretched.

Arcadio put his hands up and motioned for Forrest to come at him.

"That's enough," Stephan said and took the tablet from me, locking the screen.

My mouth dropped open. "What?" I screeched.

"You can find out who the winner is after our walk," he said and set the tablet on the dresser. "Come on, let's go."

Grumbling about rude men stealing all my fun, I followed him to the backdoor while carrying Paige.

Paige smacked my shoulder a couple times while babbling.

"See, she agrees," I grumbled. "You men are incorrigible." I nuzzled my nose against Paige's cheek. "Thank you for siding with me. Girls have to stick together. Don't worry; I'll protect you from your ridiculous fathers."

Stephan chuckled and leaned against my shoulder as he looked down at Paige. "Don't listen to your mother. She's just crabby because I ruined her fun today. You'll be just as, or more, spoiled than her, although that'll be hard to do."

"I'm not spoiled," I argued, but it was a total lie. I was spoiled as fuck.

Stephan pushed open the door and held it open with his foot. "Don't worry, son. You'll be spoiled, too. Just in a different way than your mother."

"At least until you're older. No weapons until you're at least seven," I said with a nod.

Stephan strapped Paige and Callen into the double stroller, pulled the shade halfway down so they would be shaded but still able to see, and started pushing it. "I doubt you'll be able to get everyone else to agree to that. Especially their Aunt Erina."

Laughing, I shook my head. My two best friends were wives of mafia bosses as well, and as crazy as I was.

Erina was the one who'd given me my thigh holster with knives that wouldn't be detected by metal detectors. It was the exact one she had and worked great when wearing sexy dresses to events.

"You're probably right," I agreed.

The garden was mostly shaped shrubbery and roses. There was one area with sunflowers that was my favorite. Stephan had ordered a cement bench in front of the sunflowers so I could sit and look at them.

We walked in silence for a bit, and I glanced over at him. He was incredibly handsome and intelligent, and the fact that he was so kind made him the complete package. I was unbelievably lucky to be his wife.

"You're staring," he said and glanced at me.

"I'm allowed to stare at my husband," I said.

"Something's on your mind, Amelia. What is it?"

I waited until we were in front of the sunflowers and sat on the bench with a sigh. "I don't know. I just have a bad feeling about this trip."

Stephan turned the stroller towards us and sat beside me. "That's understandable. After all, this isn't just a pleasure trip. We've got business to handle, which always comes with its own set of problems and potential dangers."

Torrence "Toupee" Malone had called in a debt that Forrest owed him. We were going there so Forrest could do this, but none of us were really sure what the job would be.

The uncertainty of it terrified me.

"Well, will it help if I tell you that we all have a present waiting for you the day we arrive?" Stephan asked.

My eyes lit up, my mouth dropped, and I nodded. "Yes! What is it? Is it jewelry? Is it a car? Is it a pool boy?"

Stephan doubled over laughing and shook his head. "You always surprise me when you respond to things. I never know what to expect."

"It's part of my charm," I said with a shrug.

"A pool boy?" he asked and shook his head. "Five of us isn't enough?"

"Well, none of you parade around the pool shirtless," I pouted. "Even Erina's husbands do that."

Stephan arched a brow. "So, now you're comparing us to Erina and Marlee's husbands?"

I turned to face him more, sitting almost sideways on the bench. "You do know that's what women do when we get together, right? We talk about our lives, complain about our husbands, boast about our husbands, and compare our lives. I know you, Brian, and Connor do the same thing. Don't even try to hide it. Erina videotaped you guys."

Stephan chuckled and leaned over to kiss me lightly on the lips. "I don't know why I expect you to act differently than I would when you and I are so similar, and you have access to my resources now."

I blinked dumbly up at him. "We're similar? You and me?"

He nodded and rested his hand against my cheek while smiling softly at me. "You don't give yourself enough credit, Amelia. You're just as smart as me, if not smarter, and are great at utilizing the resources at your disposal."

The fact that he thought so highly of me brought tears to my eyes, and I sniffled. "You're such a flatterer."

"I'm serious. You're an amazing woman, and I am truly blessed to have you as my wife. The five of us are so fucking lucky to have you in our lives." He pulled me into a hug and kissed the top of my head. "I would burn the world to the ground if it made you happy."

"I mean, I could think of a few places we could burn, but I haven't seen much of the world yet, so I'd prefer you didn't burn too much just yet." The words were mumbled into his chest as a few tears slid down my cheek. I wrapped my arms around his back, hugging him tightly so he didn't let go of me.

Stephan laughed softly. "I suppose I should let you see the world before we burn it."

"There you guys are," Forrest said, breaking our moment.

Stephan kept an arm around my shoulders as he turned to look at Forrest. "You won?"

Forrest smiled. "You know it."

Oh, right, the fight to take me on a date.

"Well, I guess you have one last person to fight then," Stephan said and stood.

My mouth dropped open, and I was sure my eyes popped at least an inch out of my skull. "What?"

Stephan stretched his neck from side to side. "It's been a long time since I've shown these egotistical punks why I'm the boss. Besides, I've planned a great date, and I can't let Forrest show me up just yet."

"As if your surprise isn't going to show up everything else," Forrest muttered.

They were torturing me with this surprise. That's exactly what this was.

"I'm not pulling my punches this time," Forrest warned Stephan. "I'm serious about taking her out."

"You can take her out when we get to Scotland," Stephan said. "Or, you can put your money where your mouth is and show me in the ring."

"Let's do this," Forrest said and puffed out his chest. "Just don't blame me if you're bruised."

"Not his face!" I shouted after them.

The two men walked away, ignoring me and teasing each other as they walked.

I looked at Paige and Callen, sound asleep in their stroller.

"Your daddies are such weird men. Let's get you inside and to your swings. I know as soon as I set you in your cribs, you will jolt awake and cry. The swing will, hopefully, let you nap more. That way, I can go on a date with one of your dads and maybe learn to separate myself from you for more than three hours."

Slowly and carefully, I made my way to the house and the living room, where Mom, Randolph, and Stanley watched a movie.

"My husbands are still fighting, but Paige and Callen are asleep. Can I leave them here in their swing with you three?"

Mom nodded. "You don't even need to ask."

"I'm sure one of my husbands will be here soon to take over childcare duties, but I don't want to make any promises." Slowly and carefully, I took them out of the stroller and put them in the swing, turning them on slow and letting them lean almost all the way back, almost flat.

They both snored softly as they continued to sleep.

Stephan walked into the room, shirt off and covered in sweat, with a huge smile on his face. "You've got thirty minutes to get ready for our date. Wear something comfortable like jeans and a t-shirt."

CHAPTER THREE

Peeking around the corner of the crate that I sat behind, I did my best to stay hidden while searching for my enemy. He was around the corner, but I could see him searching for me. I'd already been hit twice, and I couldn't take a third. It was now or never. I had to take him down. Jumping out from behind the crate, I yelled, getting his attention and making him turn. I shot him in the chest with a quick squeeze of my finger, making his vest light up bright red.

"Boo yeah!" I yelled. "Winner winner chicken dinner."

"Damn it," Stephan snapped and let his gun fall to his side. "How do you always beat me at this?"

"Because I'm the best in the land, the best mobsterina that exists." I skipped over and kissed him lightly on the lips.

Stephan put his arm around my waist and smiled wide. "You truly are. So, Mobsterina, where do you want to go eat? I can get us into any restaurant you want."

"Even wearing jeans?" I asked and looked down at our incredibly casual clothes.

He arched a brow, "Really, Amelia?"

Right, he was Stephan Moriarty, billionaire extraordinaire, sexiest man in the country, and a genius.

"*Travinso*," I answered after a moment. It was an Italian place that had opened and had a waitlist eight months out.

He smirked. "You're testing me, aren't you?"

I put a hand to my chest and dropped my mouth open. "I would never."

We walked out of the laser gun range and turned our equipment into the teenager currently running it.

"Thank you," Stephan said and handed him a one-hundred-dollar bill. "I appreciate your discretion."

"Thank you, sir," the teenager said and dipped his head. "We appreciate your patronage."

We came here once every three months and paid extra to get the area to ourselves. We also tipped the attendees for not telling the paparazzi we were here.

Stephan put his phone up to his ear while I grabbed my purse and jackets from the locker area.

When I'd grabbed it all and come out, he beamed proudly.

"Got us a reservation?" I guessed.

"They'll give us a table as soon as we get there," he said and held out his hand. "Ready, my love?"

I took his offered hand and nodded. "So hungry!"

Shea waited outside the laser gun range, his black suit, and sunglasses on as he took on bodyguard duty for the night. No one tried to come near the entrance, casting wary glances his way and whispering as they walked by. "Are you ready to leave?" he asked.

We both nodded.

"We're going to dinner now," Stephan explained.

Shea nodded and opened the door of the building for us. "Understood."

Once outside, he opened the door of our SUV that they'd let us leave parked right out front despite it being a fire zone. The perks of being rich and famous.

Once we were all inside and headed out of the parking lot, Shea asked, "Who won?"

"Who do you think?" I laughed.

"I don't know how she does it," Stephan said and sighed. "I can never beat her."

"Don't feel bad, boss. I think Arcadio is the only one who can."

"Dane and I are tied right now," I admitted angrily. "I'm going to win next time."

"Where are we going?" Shea asked.

"*Travinso*," Stephan answered.

Shea smirked and merged into traffic. "She's been drooling over their Instagram for weeks."

Stephan turned to me with a scowl. "Why didn't you mention it sooner?"

I shrugged. "I don't like taking advantage of your fame."

Both Shea and Stephan sighed.

"It's not just my fame now, love. You're just as capable of getting a reservation there as I am," Stephan said.

I blinked at him like a deer with headlights coming at it on the freeway. "Huh?"

"Kitten, you're Stephan Moriarty's wife. You could walk into any business you want and demand their finest table, and they'd kick people out so you could sit there." Shea smiled. "You're a celebrity now, too, whether you like it or not."

Since I hadn't really left the house much since our wedding, I hadn't considered it. The only time I did leave the house was with Shea to the bar, and that had been a different type of fame.

"You'll get used to it. I bet Erina and Marlee have tips for you," he added.

I text them in our group chat immediately.

Me: Did you know that we could get reservations at places simply for being married to the guys we're married to?

Erina: *Sigh* I have so much to teach you.

Marlee: LOL. Girl, duh. How do you think I get prime shopping appointments?

Me: I didn't think about it, I guess.

Erina: There's actually a new restaurant opening, Laboratory Ten, *that I was hoping we could all go to next weekend. Its grand opening is supposed to be full of top celebrities, and the food sounds great.*

Me: Sign me up.

Marlee: As long as the drinks are good, I don't care.

Erina: I say we crash it and walk up without a reservation. Make them sweat and kick out some lower-level celebrity.

Me: That's cruel, even for you, Erina.

Marlee: No, it's pretty on par for her.

Erina: Fine, I'll make a reservation for the three of us. They'll let us bring two bodyguards, so Marlee tell Brian we've got it covered, and Amelia and I will bring one of our husbands.

Marlee: You know he won't go for that. I'll bring my bodyguard.

Erina: What's new with you, Amelia? How are my niece and nephew?

Me: I just defeated Stephan in another laser tag match.

Erina: That's my girl!

Marlee: You two are weird.

Me: Oh, and Callen finally crawled!

Erina & Marlee: Yay!

Me: So, next Saturday, what time? Remember I can't be out too late because we're leaving for Scotland Sunday.

Erina: You'll sleep on the plane anyway.

Marlee: And they have bags for throwing up.

She sent a throwing up emoji, and I laughed loudly, making Stephan and Shea look at me.

"The girls are being themselves," I said with a shrug of one shoulder.

"Making plans?" Stephan asked.

I narrowed my eyes at him. "Were you looking over my shoulder?"

He showed me his phone, where Brian and Connor were in a group chat with him. They were discussing the restaurant Erina had mentioned. "Nope."

I should have known.

"Is it okay for me to go out the night before our trip?" I asked.

Stephan nodded as he responded to a message. "Yeah, but who are you going to take?"

"Arcadio hasn't guarded me in a while," I commented and tapped my lip.

"You're taking me," Shea said.

"You can't always bodyguard me," I reminded him. "You're supposed to be Stephan's main bodyguard, remember?"

Shea growled, and his grip on the steering wheel tightened.

"We should consider getting her her own bodyguard," Stephan said.

We had interviewed a few people, but Shea, Forrest, and Dane had shot them all down.

"I don't know why you guys are opposed to it," I commented. "If I chose one of you as my guard, the others would think I was picking a favorite, and I don't want any discord between us."

The last thing I needed was strife in our personal lives.

Shea sighed. "You're right, but it still makes me worry to have someone who isn't us guarding you."

"Since I'm the boss's wife, do I get the power to tell them what to do?" I asked Stephan quietly.

Stephan smiled and nodded. "Yep."

"I want a bodyguard, and I will interview them. You five can put them through tests, physical ones, mental ones, whatever, but I get the final say."

Stephan cleared his throat.

I rolled my eyes. "Fine, Stephan gets the ultimate final say."

Stephan relaxed into his seat with a nod and resumed messaging.

"It has to be someone already in the mafia," I commented.

"And he has to be ugly," Shea added.

Stephan chuckled. "But then, how will Amelia live out her pool boy fantasies?"

Shea slammed on the brakes a little too hard at the red light and jerked around in his seat to look at us. "What!"

I glared at Stephan, who ignored us to continue messaging.

"I was teasing Stephan. He's just trying to get me in trouble with you now."

At a red light, Shea pulled out his phone and started messaging someone.

"How many group chats am I not in?" I asked curiously.

"Seven," Shea answered.

My mouth dropped. "You know the exact number?"

"We talked about how upset you would be to realize you weren't part of these chats. We've got a chat with all five of us, one without Stephan, one without Dane, one without Forrest, one without Arcadio, and one with all of Erina's men except Connor. I've got one that's just Stephan and me."

There were likely even more chats I wasn't part of, ones Shea also wasn't part of. So many jokes I wasn't involved in.

I pouted. "Rude."

We pulled up to the restaurant, and there were tons of paparazzi there snapping pictures of people going inside.

I shined my wedding ring on my shirt and waited for Shea to open the door for Stephan and then for Stephan to open the door for me.

Accepting his hand, I let him help me out of the SUV and onto a red carpet.

What kind of ritzy place was this? I knew it catered to the wealthy, but a red carpet? Really?

Stephan slipped his arm around my waist, pulled me close, and plastered on his playboy smile as he posed for the cameras.

I smiled as well, playing my part as his wife, now used to the schmoozing necessary to be in public together.

They called out questions, but Stephan and I ignored them all, just smiling as we walked into the restaurant.

The maître d' smiled warmly. "Mister and Missus Moriarty, it is so kind of you to visit our establishment. We have a table ready for you this way."

After grabbing two menus, he led the three of us to a table in the back of the restaurant. I looked at the table next to us and put my hands on my hips. "Really?"

Erina looked up from the menu she was inspecting, saw me, and threw her head back as she laughed.

"Can we put these two tables together?" Connor requested.

The maître d' nodded and snapped his fingers.

Three men in tuxedos ran over and immediately reconfigured the two two-person tables into a single four-person table.

I sat down beside Erina and hugged her. "You bitch. Did you put some surveillance on us or something?"

Connor chuckled. "No, this was actually my idea. I had no idea you were coming here, though."

I narrowed my eyes suspiciously, which made Connor smile wider.

"Drinks?" a waiter asked us.

"She'll have the same as me," Erina answered.

"And Mr. Moriarty will have the same as me," Connor replied.

Knowing Erin and Connor, the drinks would be tasty, so there was no reason to argue.

Stephan nodded at the waiter, and he took off to the back.

Shea walked behind us to where one of Erina's other husbands, Blain, stood on bodyguard duty. They bumped fists and then stood with hands clasped in front of them.

"Did you tell Stephan about our plans?" Erina asked.

"No, because your husband beat me to it," I answered.

Erina's eyes widened, and she looked at Connor. "You ass."

Connor chuckled. "It's not often I get to one-up them, darling, so don't get too angry."

"He read over your shoulder again?" I guessed. Erina had an issue with not paying attention to her back when she was texting, and I told her she had to stop that or she'd end up dead.

Erina sighed. "Yeah, yeah, I know."

"So, rumor is that our niece and nephew are both crawling now?" Connor asked.

I nodded and beamed with pride. "Yes! I was so proud of Callen."

"It won't be long before we've got them on the archery range," Erina said.

Stephan looked at me over the top of his water glass, silently reminding me of our recent discussion.

"No weapons," I said and glared at Erina.

She put a hand to her heart. "As if I would put those adorable children in harm's way. You wound me."

"It's plastic," Connor said. "And she dulled the edges herself."

"Your drinks," the waiter said as he set drinks down for all four of us.

I raised mine. "To a prosperous year."

They all clinked their glasses against mine.

"So, there are rumors about your trip," Connor said softly. His eyes didn't leave the menu, but I knew he was paying close attention to us, watching for body language as well as words.

"There are always rumors," Stephan commented, his posture still relaxed and calm, a mirror of Connor.

I glanced at Erina, who discreetly shrugged one shoulder as we drank from our drinks.

"You need backup?" Connor asked and raised his eyes to look at Stephan over the top of his menu.

My body tensed. Did he know something I didn't? Was there more danger expected on this trip than the guys were letting me in on?

Stephan smiled and set his closed menu on top of the table. "I appreciate the offer, but no, we should be fine."

Connor set his menu down, too, and leaned forward, his hands clasped on top of the closed menu. "Don't do something stupid, Stephan. If you notice things aren't as they seem, call us. We'll fly there immediately."

Stephan reached over and set his hand on my knee. "It will be okay, but I really do appreciate the offer, and if things spiral into that state, I will contact you."

Connor sat back, picked his drink up, and smiled. "Good."

"You know what we need?" Erina asked me.

"What?" I asked, and took a long drink from my glass.

"A girls' weekend. Like, a full weekend without any of them," she answered.

I scoffed. "As if that could ever happen."

She looked at Connor. "Mafia Weekend, I want Amelia, Marlee, and I to have full access to the casino with none of you around. You understand? All of you at the mafia event while we are all at the casino. None of our husbands around. Only bodyguards, which we will let you pick, but they can't come into certain rooms with us. We won't lock the doors on them, but they have to stand outside. Agreed?"

Mafia Weekend was a year away, but we had to plan events like this so far in advance, or the guys would go crazy. I was already worried about Mafia Weekend because it was when all of the mafia bosses in this country gathered to discuss agreements and issues as well as any federal investigations the others should be aware of. A weekend away with my two favorite women would be a good distraction; I just hoped I'd be more comfortable with leaving the kids by then.

Connor narrowed his eyes and tapped his pointer finger on his glass as he thought. "One night," he countered.

She looked at me, and I gave a slight dip of my head. "Fine, one night."

He looked at Stephan. "Agreed?"

Stephan sighed. "Amelia would just find a way to lose her tail or knock them unconscious anyway, so yes."

I leaned over and kissed his cheek. "You really do know me."

He shook his head. "And you call us incorrigible."

"We'll work everything out," Connor agreed. "Promise you won't leave the casino?"

Erina and I nodded. "We won't have a reason to leave it. You think any of the nearby casinos are better than ours?" Her brow arched as she asked the question, taunting Connor.

Connor scoffed. "None of those casinos hold a candle to ours."

Erina smiled wide. "Exactly, so we will stay in the casino and enjoy ourselves while you all argue and have dick-measuring contests."

I'd been mid-drink and spit it out, thankfully back into the glass, but the alcohol burned my throat, and Erina had to pat my back to help me stop coughing.

"Easy, girl," Erina teased me.

"So, what are you most excited about for this trip?" Connor asked me.

"The castles!" I exclaimed.

"You mean yours?" Connor asked.

"It's Stephan's," I corrected. "I know we're married, but still, it's his."

Stephan took a long drink from his glass. "She's infuriating."

"Give her a few years," Connor said with a soft smile, reached across the table, and took Erina's hand. "They don't like to accept things because they are such strong, independent women."

"It's part of why you love us," Erina said as she took his hand and squeezed it with a smile.

"Aw, you two are so freaking cute," I crooned.

"I'm glad you're past your honeymoon phase, finally," Erina commented as she looked at us. "You two were practically in each other's laps all of the time."

"Were not," I countered with a slight blush.

Stephan draped an arm across the back of my chair and smiled wide. "If she were yours, you'd do the same."

"Are you ready to order?" the waiter asked as he came back over.

"Yes," Stephan answered.

———

By the time we left the restaurant, I was drunk, overly full, and my face hurt from laughing so much.

Stephan kept his arm around my waist as we walked out to the waiting SUV and carried the leftovers and extra food I'd bought for Shea.

When we finally got into the SUV, I sighed and patted my stomach. "That was delicious. We should definitely come back here again."

"Yeah, this place definitely lived up to the hype for once," Stephan said and exhaled. "If we come back too often, I'll have to up my workout routine."

"You mean I get to eat delicious food more *and* see a shirtless, sweaty Stephan more? Count me in!" I shouted.

Shea and Stephan laughed.

We headed toward home, and I relaxed. "I got you food," I told Shea.

"Thank you," he said. "I thought you might just be ordering

more for when you got home."

"I'd thought about it," I admitted. "But it was cruel to make you stand nearby to see and smell the food but not get any of it. So, I thought getting an extra order would be nice."

"I appreciate you," Shea said.

"So very thoughtful," Stephan agreed.

"Do you think we *should* ask Connor and the guys to go with us?" I asked Stephan, turning to the side to look at him.

He smiled, rested his hand gently on my cheek, and said, "There's nothing to worry about. We will handle it."

"There's always something to worry about," I mumbled and leaned into his hand. "You forget that I attract danger."

Both laughed again.

"Oh, we haven't forgotten," Stephan said. "It is something we almost always consider when we go places. Truthfully, I expected something to happen at dinner tonight, so I was pleasantly surprised when we had a nice, quiet evening."

My mouth dropped open, but I quickly shut it. "Yeah, honestly, me too."

"Even though you do bring lots of trouble, you also have a way of bringing people together. I'd been trying for years to get Connor to agree to a partnership, and it ended up just taking you meeting his wife to do it. Now, he and I are friends, and our partnership is much stronger than it would have been had you not come into our lives."

"You've done nothing but strengthen our lives," Shea added. "Even with the extra chaos you tend to bring."

"Seriously, who robs a fucking bar?" Stephan asked and shook his head.

The three of us laughed together, and I let it ease the worry in my gut.

CHAPTER FOUR

After a grueling fifteen-hour flight, we finally made it to Scotland.

Having five husbands definitely helped when it came to dealing with the twins. Had I been on my own, I probably would have gone crazy by the time the plane landed.

Also, flying in our private jet helped a lot since we could walk around, and there was no one to complain when the babies cried.

"We'll be there soon," Stephan promised. He put his arm around my shoulders and pulled me until my head rested on his chest. "Close your eyes and rest."

"It's dark," I huffed with annoyance. "I can't see anything." I hadn't realized that our flight was going to land at night, which meant I wasn't going to be able to see anything in the daytime until tomorrow. My first view of the castle would be in the dark.

As if reading my thoughts, Stephan squeezed me. "There are lots of lights, so you'll still be able to see the castle; we'll hold an umbrella over you so the rain won't get in your face while you gawk at it."

"I'm being a brat, I know. Sorry," I whispered and yawned.

"It's okay. We're all tired. We understand," he said. "If I were you, I'd be sad I didn't get to see the castle during the daytime as well, so don't feel too bad about it."

Our driver had an incredibly thick accent that made it hard to understand him. Forrest didn't seem to have any issues understanding him, though, which made me even more curious about his past here.

We hadn't really had any time to talk, but I was determined to get some information out of him soon.

What felt like two hours later, we finally arrived, and I was already gawking.

The castle was gorgeous, even with the rain falling all around it.

I smooshed my face up against the glass window of the SUV and said, "It's perfect."

"Wait until you see the inside," Shea said.

"And the garden!" the driver said.

"There's a garden?" I asked.

"Ay, one of the most beautiful in this area," he said with a nod and glanced at me in the rearview mirror. "It's been a long time since we've had such a pretty and young baroness if you don't mind my saying so, hen."

Hen? Had he called me hen just now? And he'd toned his accent down a ton. I could actually understand him.

"I'm not a baroness," I said with a chuckle. "Though, I wouldn't mind a title like that." It would go well with my mobsterina title.

Stephan cleared his throat, making the driver look at him, but I ignored them to see what transpired.

"My apologies; I guess I misheard the rumors floating around the area," he said after a second, his voice softer.

"Let's get the babies inside," Stephan said, interrupting our conversation.

"Make sure you pull the cover down tight," I ordered.

Shea and Arcadio were already doing that very thing.

"Once you open the doors, I will help bring the luggage in," the driver said. "Don't want it sitting in the rain."

"Does it ever stop raining?" I asked.

He smiled. "Rarely, but when it does, oh, it's gorgeous."

I loved the rain, but sightseeing was much easier in the sun.

"Wait here," Stephan said. "I'll get the door open, and then you and the babies can come. I don't want you standing in the rain."

"Okay," I agreed.

Stephan climbed out of the SUV, shutting the door quickly behind him. Forrest and Dane went with him to open the front door, Dane holding an umbrella for Stephan.

I rubbed my arms against the chill that had come in when Stephan opened the door.

"Don't worry, we had a ton of blankets delivered ahead of our arrival," Arcadio said.

Shea leaned close to whisper in my ear. "Plus, I'll keep you plenty warm tonight." He pulled back and winked at me.

"Don't complain about my icicle toes between your thighs then." I gave him a return wink.

Arcadio and Shea laughed, knowing damn well I was being serious. It wasn't my fault I had poor circulation, and my toes were always cold.

"There is some staff here as well, and I'm sure they've already started the fires in the fireplaces," Arcadio added.

Right, no central heating and air in a castle. That was something I wasn't sure I would like, but for the right to live in a castle, I would accept it.

Dane opened the door and smiled at me. "Come on, beautiful. Let's get you out of this vehicle so you can gawk at the castle a bit and then head indoors."

Forrest walked to the other side of the vehicle and held another umbrella. "I'll escort you and Paige," he said to Arcadio.

"I'll come back to get you and Callen," Dane told Shea.

Shea nodded and smiled at me. "Go on."

Dane held out his hand, and I took it as I stepped out of the SUV. A wind gust hit me, making me shiver, but I ignored it as I looked up at the stone castle. It really was gorgeous.

The rain stopped, allowing me to step out from under the umbrella to really look at it.

Stephan walked over, smiling wide. "Remember that surprise I told you about?"

I nodded, still taking in the sight of the castle. "Yes."

"This castle," he said, as he bent to whisper in my ear, "is yours."

My head whipped to the side to look at him; I heard it crack but ignored the pain. "Say that again?"

He kissed me lightly on the lips. "You, Mrs. Moriarty, are the sole owner of this castle." He set an iron key into my hand with a small red bow tied to it.

My mouth dropped open. "Y-you bought me a castle?"

"Actually, we all chipped in," Dane said.

I spun to look at him. "What?"

He had closed the umbrella since the rain had stopped and was using it like a cane now. "We made Stephan split the cost between us all. This castle was purchased equally amongst us for you."

My husbands had bought me a castle.

Tears streamed down my cheeks, and I sniffled. They'd bought me a freaking castle.

"This is our wedding present to you," Forrest said from behind me.

I turned around to face him. "I didn't get any of you guys a present."

He stepped forward, smiled, and rested his hand on my cheek. "Honey, you marrying us was the only present we needed. Then, you went and blessed us with two beautiful children."

Looking back up at the castle, I looked at it with new eyes. It wasn't Stephan's…it was mine.

"So, remember a year or so ago when you were worried about not having a place of your own if we decided to separate?" Arcadio asked as he joined us. "Well, now you can escape from us to your own castle if you ever did leave."

"She is not leaving us," Shea growled.

He actually growled!

I looked around at my husbands and screeched, "You bought me a castle!" The reality hit me, and I quickly jumped up to kiss each of them on the lips. "Erina is going to be so jealous! Thank you. Thank you. Thank you."

Stephan put his arm around my shoulders and led me into the castle. "Come on, let's get inside. You're shivering even if you are excited, and I don't want you to get sick and not be able to sightsee."

"Does this mean I can have parties and stuff here?" I asked him.

He chuckled. "It's your place, Amelia. You can do whatever

47

you want here. Want to have a girls' night? Want to throw a rave? This is your place; you can do whatever you want."

"A rave does sound fun," I said and tapped my pointer finger against my lips.

He squeezed my shoulders. "I bet it does."

The inside was even better than I could have imagined, and I spent an hour squealing as I toured it and looked at everything.

Shea had to throw me over his shoulder and carry me to the room he'd chosen as his and force me to go to sleep.

Once I was under the heavy blankets with Shea wrapped around me, it wasn't hard to fall asleep.

I woke up bright and early and immediately ran over to throw the curtains back to let the sunlight in. "It's sunny!" I screeched.

Shea groaned. "Really, Amelia?"

"We're going sightseeing today, right?" I asked as I ran back to the bed and climbed beneath the covers with him. It was cold out there!

"Yes," Shea answered, his eyes still closed.

"I'm hungry," I complained and stuck my lip out in a pout.

"Stop pouting." He hadn't even opened his eyes.

With a groan, I flopped over onto him. "I'm withering away!" Rolling back and forth made him groan, and he pushed me off after another few seconds.

"Fine, I'm awake." He stood and stretched, giving me a view of his broad, muscular back and large, round butt.

"Dat ass," I mumbled and wiped my hand across my mouth to wipe up the drool.

Shea looked over his shoulder and smiled. "Let's get downstairs. I guarantee Stephan is already awake and on his second cup of coffee."

My suitcase sat against the wall, and Shea quickly set it on the bed and opened it for me so I didn't have to get out from beneath the covers just yet.

"You really do love me," I whispered as I took out clothes. Instead of putting them on right away, I put them beneath the covers with me to warm up.

"I really do," he agreed with a nod and got dressed.

"I need house slippers with fur lining so I don't have to walk on the cold floor to go pee in the middle of the night," I commented. "Hopefully, I can find some when we're out on our sightseeing trip."

"If we can't find a pair today, we will order some," Shea promised. "I want a pair, and my size is rarely in stock at places."

I glanced down at his big feet and smirked. "I'm not complaining."

He laughed and shook his head.

My clothes were warm enough for me to get dressed, which I did quickly and then hurried to the bathroom to brush my teeth and hair.

As I finished brushing my hair, I heard Callen crying. Tossing the brush down, I darted out of the bathroom and down the hallway, following the sounds of his distress.

Forrest held Callen in his arms and bounced him. "It's okay, buddy. You're fine."

"What happened?" I asked as I walked over.

Callen turned in Forrest's arms at my voice and cried harder.

"He's playing it up for you," Forrest said. "He was on the floor and let his head drop to the ground a bit too hard. There's not even a bump."

I took Callen from Forrest and kissed all across his forehead, especially over the little red spot. "Poor baby. It's okay. You're hard-headed like your mama."

"Ma. Ma," Callen said through sniffles.

My mouth dropped, and I looked up at Forrest, who had wide eyes. "He...he said it, right? I didn't imagine it?"

"He said mama," Forrest said and nodded. "I heard it, too."

I squeezed Callen and squealed softly. "You finally called me mama."

"Mama. Ma. Ma. Mama," Callen said repeatedly.

"Forrest," I said, and raised my head to tell him to record it, but he already had his cell phone out, a huge smile on his face as he recorded us.

"What's going on?" Shea asked as he came inside. "I heard Callen crying."

"He said mama!" I shouted and squeezed Callen again.

"I got it on video," Forrest said.

"Show me," Shea ordered and walked up to Forrest's side.

"Ma. Ma. Mamamama," Callen said.

Shea smiled wide, and I swore tears shone in his eyes. "Wow."

"We have to tell the others!" I said quickly and walked out of the room, but then froze, unsure which direction to go or where the others were.

Forrest had Paige in his arms and smiled down at me. "Come on, this way."

"I'll memorize the layout soon," I grumbled.

We walked down the hallway, to a set of stairs, which we descended carefully, and then down another hallway until we reached a dining room.

The dining room was fully furnished with a plush red carpet beneath the table.

Stephan and Dane sat at the table drinking coffee and

reading on their tablets. They both looked up when we came in.

"Guys!" I shouted, but was interrupted by Callen.

"Mamamamamama," he babbled.

Dane and Stephan's eyes widened, and then they both smiled.

"Such a smart boy," Stephan praised.

"Now, if only Paige would say Dada," Forrest said as he bounced her in his arms.

She babbled a ton of vowel sounds but hadn't said consonants yet.

"Are you hungry?" Stephan asked.

I nodded while bouncing Callen in my arms. "Mama is super hungry." I nuzzled my nose against his chubby little cheek. "Hungry."

Callen blew a raspberry and said something in baby gibberish.

"I think that means he's hungry, too," Arcadio said from the doorway. "I'll get their food ready."

"The chef is preparing breakfast for us," Stephan informed me. "Why don't you sit?"

"Sit? How can I possibly sit when my baby boy finally said my name?" I said and danced around the room with Callen.

"What's your plan for the day?" Stephan asked as he continued to sip his coffee.

"We're going sightseeing, right?" I asked, and stopped to look at everybody.

"I'm afraid I won't be going," Forrest said.

Narrowing my eyes, I walked up to him and asked, "Why not?"

He fidgeted. "I have to meet up with Toupee."

"You're not going alone, right?" I swallowed hard.

Forrest sighed and held Paige out to Shea, who took her immediately. Forrest set his hand on my shoulder. "Honey, I've got to meet with him. No, I won't be alone. Arcadio is going with me."

I looked at Stephan. "You're his boss. Can't you force Toupee to allow us to be there?"

Stephan smiled. "Darling, this is Forrest's past. I trust his judgment on this."

"I don't," I whispered. "He hasn't told me anything about it." I dared a glance up at Forrest and saw that he was frowning and looked...sad.

"I don't like bringing up the past," he admitted. "I will tell you more tonight, though, okay?"

"Promise?" I asked.

He nodded. "Promise."

"If something happens, I will blow up this fucking continent. You know that, right?"

Forrest bent and kissed me lightly on the lips, our lips barely touching. "I know, honey. I know. Toupee doesn't want to kill me. He could have sent someone to do that instead of making me come here. This is different."

I didn't like it. Not one fucking bit. Something was going on, and I didn't know what it was or how to prepare for it.

Dane took Callen from me. "Let's go feed you, little man."

Forrest took my hand and pulled me out of the dining room and to a nearby room that seemed to be a living room, but it was obvious no one had used it in a very long time. The room had two doors that slid out from the wall and locked with a little lock. Forrest turned and immediately crushed me against him in a hug. "I promise, this will be okay. I promise that nothing bad will happen to me."

"You can't promise that," I mumbled into his shirt and

clung to him, my hands gripping the back of his shirt as if that could keep him safe with me. "We're mafia; things never go according to plan."

"He won't risk Stephan's wrath," Forrest assured me. "He knows Stephan isn't all talk and knows that my brothers would come for revenge."

"I'll skin them all," I swore.

He chuckled and pushed me back to look down at me, a huge smile on his face. "I'll warn him my wife is even crazier than my brothers."

"Promise you'll be extra careful?"

He nodded and kissed me passionately, his tongue and mine dancing together for several minutes before he pulled back. "You think I'm going to give up these kisses? Not on your life, ma'am. I will fight a million unicorns if I have to."

I'd forgotten Scotland's national animal was the unicorn until he said that. A smile lit up my face, and I wrapped my arms around his neck. "Only a million?"

Forrest laughed and kissed the tip of my nose. "When I come home, I'll show you just how much I cherish you."

"I'll hold you to that." I rested my head against his chest. "Your babies need you. I need you."

He squeezed me. "I'll always come home, Amelia. I can promise you that."

No, no, he could not, but I accepted the statement for what it was.

"I love you, Forrest."

"I love you, too, Amelia."

After another kiss that stole my breath, we rejoined the others and found breakfast on the table, waiting for us.

Breakfast was lively as the guys argued over who Paige

would call dada first. I knew it was just their rivalry, and no actual hard feelings would be had despite their teasing.

My stomach felt like it was full of lead as we sat there, but I forced myself to drink in every detail, every memory, just in case something did happen.

Forrest left with a kiss on my cheek, and then Stephan stood and held his hand out to me.

"You sure?" I whispered again.

Stephan took my hand and patted the back of it. "Yes. Let's go sightsee and enjoy our day seeing a new place, shopping at new stores, and test just how much money one woman can spend in a day."

My smile grew at his challenge. "Oh, baby, challenge accepted."

"Do you want us all to go?" Dane asked. "I was thinking about staying here with the babies so you could sightsee easier."

"You sure?" I asked.

He nodded. "I've been here several times, and while I'd love to see you spend a ton of Stephan's money, I think it'll make you a little less stressed to enjoy your day without the kiddos in tow."

Taking the babies would definitely change the day because I would be more worried about them and keeping them warm, diapers clean, and happy than spending the time thoroughly shopping my heart out. "I appreciate you so much," I whispered and kissed him.

"Remember that tonight when you come home." He winked and then shoved me with one hand towards the door. "Go on, enjoy your day."

"I'll bring you home a gift," I promised as I headed towards the hallway.

"I prefer pink lace," he called out.

I snickered. "Pink lace speedo for Dane. Got it."

"Oh, I'm totally buying him one for his birthday now," Shea whispered as we headed towards the front door.

Stephan chuckled. "He so set himself up for that."

"I'm buying him a thong if I don't find a speedo today," I said with a devilish smirk.

Shea and Stephan laughed and shook their heads.

The drive took longer than I expected, but I didn't mind one bit as I looked at the beautiful scenery around us. Everything was so green! The ocean was beautiful, too.

When we made it to the city, Shea quickly found a place to park, and we all climbed out.

"Walking is much easier in this city than driving," he explained as he locked the SUV.

"It's also easier because we are less likely to be recognized, right?" I commented as we started walking down the street.

I linked my hand with Stephan's, Shea walking right behind us.

"Stephan might get recognized by someone, but yes, it is far less likely," Shea agreed.

"I'm so glad it's sunny today," Stephan said. "I was worried when we arrived yesterday."

I smiled up at him. "I just had to bring some of my sun with me."

He smiled down and brushed his thumb over my cheek. "You do bring sunshine with you wherever you go."

We started to walk by a store with pretty dresses inside, but I stopped and turned back. "Here!"

Stephan chuckled. "My apologies; how dare I try to walk by such a place without first allowing you to step inside."

Shea opened the door and walked inside, doing a quick

check before coming back out and holding the door open for us. "Clear."

After we walked inside, Shea took up a spot by the door, his stance relaxed and a smile on his face, but I knew he was on high alert if anyone came near.

We walked in, and the woman at the register smiled at me. She said something, and it sounded like a nice question, but I didn't understand it. So, I just smiled and nodded once.

"She just asked how you are," Stephan explained.

I looked at him. "You speak Gaelic?"

"A little," he admitted and shrugged one shoulder.

"I should have started learning when I found out we were coming here," I admitted and sighed. "Wasted time."

"Oh, English," the woman said. "Sorry."

"Your dresses are lovely," I complimented as I looked through the various racks.

"Thank you," she replied, smiling even wider.

"This dress would look lovely on you," Stephan said and held up a pretty floral dress with long sleeves.

"Oh, that is pretty," I agreed. "I don't know what size I am, though."

The woman came over, held up the dress Stephan had had in his hand, and tilted her head to the side as she considered me. "This size should fit. Would you like to try it on just to be sure?"

I nodded. "Yes, please."

After trying the dress on and confirming that size fit, I breezed through the store, buying five dresses, each a different style and color.

Stephan didn't seem bothered by the price, not that I really knew how much it was since it wasn't the same currency we used. Still, it felt like a lot, and the woman seemed very happy with our purchases. She even wrapped them in tissue paper before putting them inside the bag.

Stephan carried the bag in his right hand while he held my hand in his left one. "You lead the way, okay? I want you to go into any store that catches your eye. Understood?"

"Okay," I agreed.

Immediately, I saw a store with jewelry and veered towards it.

Even though I was mostly shopping, I was really enjoying the different architecture, the people, and the way their language sounded. Sometimes, it was nice to be around another culture, just to soak it up and experience it, even without understanding the discussions.

We made our way around town, stopped at a beautiful cathedral to have a private tour inside, thanks to Stephan's extra tip, and even stopped at an art gallery where Stephan purchased something for my new castle.

Lunchtime hit, and I was famished.

"Food," I begged, dragging my feet slowly like I was starving.

Shea snickered. "Dramatic much?"

"There's a great pub around the block if I remember correctly," Stephan said.

"As long as there is food that is edible, I'm totally fine with it," I agreed.

We walked to the establishment, and we could hear the live music coming from the pub over half a block away.

Inside, we were given a table right away, and the boys ordered beer for themselves.

I opted for water.

Looking over the menu, I couldn't decide, so I left it up to Stephan.

There were a handful of scruffy men at the bar top who kept glancing at us.

Only two other couples were at tables, engrossed on what were definitely dates.

They were both such cute couples that I kept staring at them.

One of the men caught me staring, and when his date glanced down, he winked at me.

Shea started to stand, having seen it, but I set my hand on his forearm. "Easy, big man. He just misunderstood my attention."

"I'll set the record straight," he said.

"Ox, sit," Stephan said with a sigh.

Shea grumbled, but remained sitting.

Three of the scruffy men walked toward us, and Shea tensed, preparing for a fight.

Since we'd been going to the pub, we hadn't brought our guns with us.

We still had our knives, though, and my dagger was in the palm of my hand immediately beneath the table.

Stephan reached over and patted my thigh. "Easy, Amelia. You're just as bad as them."

"We know you?" one of the men asked Stephan.

Stephan looked up at them and squinted. "I don't think so."

"Americans?" one of them asked, though I didn't think he really needed to ask it as a question since our accents were pretty obvious.

"Yes," I answered and smiled. "It's my first time here, and I'm really enjoying this city."

"Wait, I know her," the third man said.

Shea tensed beside me.

"You're that new baroness!" he shouted suddenly.

I frowned. "What?"

Stephan frowned, too. "Why do people keep saying that?"

"You bought that castle, yeah?" one of them asked.

I nodded. "Yes, I just bought a castle." I didn't need to say I was given it.

"The papers ran an article about you. It's the first time in round bout thirty years that a foreigner has become an owner and one with a title no less."

"Wait, are you saying I'm actually a baroness?" I asked.

"Yeah, did you not receive your summons?" one of the others asked.

"Summons?" Shea asked.

"She might have to go before parliament," he explained.

My eyes widened, and when I looked at Stephan, I saw he was just as shocked as me.

"Parliament?" I asked, a bit breathless.

"Congratulations," the scruffy men all said.

"Hey, it's the new baroness!" someone shouted.

Baroness. I was really a baroness.

CHAPTER FIVE

"Why hasn't he called?" I asked as I paced the living room for the dozenth time.

It was ten o'clock at night, and Forrest still hadn't come home or called. Arcadio wasn't answering his phone either.

"It's probably just a reception issue," Shea said, trying to reassure me.

My phone in hand, I started trying to find resources to buy weapons.

Stephan set his hand over my phone and smiled. "Darling, take a deep breath."

I obeyed.

"They're fine. This isn't their first rodeo, and Forrest knows this place better than most tour guides. I know that we're getting up there in age, but ten o'clock isn't that late when it comes to running jobs."

He was right, dammit, but still.

With a sigh, I put my phone away and let my forehead drop to rest on his chest. "I'm sorry."

"I expected this to be your reaction, honestly. This is the

first time you've been away from them for more than a few hours in about a year. You're just having withdrawal symptoms, much like you do when you leave Paige and Callen. However, you need to have more faith in Arcadio and Forrest. Unlike Paige and Callen, they do know how to take care of themselves and aren't defenseless."

"I know," I whispered.

"Did you find anything else out about the baroness title?" Stephan asked Shea.

"I did," Dane answered from the couch where he had his tablet on. "I have confirmed that she did get the title when we purchased the land in her name."

"Baroness Amelia Moriarty," I said with a smile. "I like it."

"Baroness Amelia 'Mobsterina' Moriarty," Shea corrected me.

"Pretty sure this is the first time that a female mobster has been a baroness," Dane said as he continued reading whatever website he was looking at.

"Probably not," I argued. "I bet there were plenty of women running businesses behind the law's eyes before. Especially before there were surveillance cameras and other things."

"Most definitely," Stephan agreed.

"I need a distraction," I said. "Let's go out."

All three of their heads snapped around to stare at me.

"You want to go out?" Dane asked.

I nodded. "Let's go to a pub or bar or something. I still want to sightsee and take in the local people."

"You want to people watch all the drunk Scottish people and listen to their accents," Dane translated.

I pointed at him and winked. "Bingo."

"Sounds good to me," Stephan said. "There's one nearby, and we can make it home quickly if they call."

"I'll stay and babysit this time," Shea offered.

Dane slapped his hand on Shea's back. "I don't care what Amelia says about you; you're awesome."

I rolled my eyes and headed towards the door. "Let's go before I change my mind."

"Where are we going?" Forrest asked.

I spun around, ran, and jumped up to wrap my arms around his neck and legs around his waist. "Forrest!"

Forrest caught me easily while chuckling. "Hey, honey. Miss me?"

I leaned back and glared. "You weren't answering your phones."

"No service," Arcadio said as he walked in, limping.

I jumped off Forrest. "What happened? Why are you limping?"

Arcadio looked at the floor. "I don't want to talk about it."

Forrest smiled wide, clearly happy. "He tripped over a root and sprained his ankle. For a Jackal, he isn't very nimble sometimes."

Jackal was Arcadio's mafia nickname.

Dane and Shea burst into laughter.

"We're going to go to a pub; want to come?" I asked Arcadio.

He looked up with slightly wide eyes. "You're going to a pub?"

My brows pinched together. "Why is everyone so surprised at that? I like going out."

"You don't usually go out," he said. "That's all."

"Because it's expensive, and we can just drink at home,

plus, we get recognized or get hassled," I said. "No one really knows us here."

"Except for you being the new baroness," Dane reminded me.

I groaned. "Right, except for that article which put a picture of me in it."

"Wait, what? What did we miss?" Forrest asked.

"I'll explain it all over drinks," I said.

"I need a drink…or five," Arcadio said and started limping towards the front door.

I took Forrest's hand and forced him to walk at my side. "Everything okay?"

He nodded and squeezed my hand. "Yep. I'm not done yet, but things moved along nicely tonight without incident."

We climbed into the SUV, and I stayed glued to Forrest's side. "Promise you're being careful?"

He put his arm around me and pulled me against his side. I loved the way I molded against him.

"Promise."

"Let's drink!" Arcadio shouted.

"Drinks!" I shouted back and turned to high-five him.

"Are they ever going to mature beyond the twenties?" Stephan asked Dane.

Dane shook his head. "Nope."

Stephan sighed. "That's what I figured. Well, tonight, I am going to be the designated driver for our return."

Everyone stared at him in shock, including me.

"You?" I asked.

He nodded and smiled. "We are on vacation, and it's only fair that Amelia gets to go all out with her husbands at a pub tonight. I had some drinks earlier today and don't feel up to it tonight, anyway. So, I'll let you all drink instead."

"We can't leave you unprotected," Forrest argued. "At least one of us has to stay relatively sober."

"Do I really need to make this an order?" Stephan asked and arched a brow as he turned around from the passenger seat to look at us.

"I mean, I do like it when you order me around," I said and smiled.

Stephan chuckled. "Fine, I order you all to drink to your heart's content and enjoy yourselves. I will drive the SUV home tonight."

"You paying, too?" Dane asked as he started the SUV.

Stephan sighed. "Yes."

"Drinks on Stephan!" I shouted.

"Yeah!" Forrest, Dane, and Arcadio shouted back, and we took turns high-fiving each other.

"Children, all of you, I swear." Stephan shook his head, but the smile on his face betrayed his true feelings.

The pub we went to was pretty lively, and the music was loud. We, of course, drew attention, but most were already so many drinks in that they stopped paying us much mind once we got a seat and ordered drinks.

Forrest spoke the language surprisingly well, and I narrowed my eyes a bit as the female bartender spoke to him in a way that seemed like flirting.

Forrest winked at her as he took a tray of our drinks and turned to our table, only smiling wider when he saw my narrowed eyes. "You're not jealous, are you, wife?"

Hearing him call me wife was definitely on the top ten list. I sat back, took my drink, and said, "I don't know what you mean."

"Want me to pull the surveillance so you can hear what she said?" Dane offered.

Yes. "No."

"Liar," Arcadio whispered.

"So, now that I'm royalty and all," I said to change the subject.

"Pretty sure you aren't considered royalty," Forrest said quietly.

"I think I need a scepter. You know, a nice one, with gemstones, a big diamond, and all that," I continued instead of acknowledging him. "Nothing too obscene, but still one befitting me and my new title."

"Good thing you stole a crown during the cruise, or we'd have to buy you that, too," Arcadio muttered.

"I did not steal the crown. They just never came to claim it." I shrugged a shoulder. "I couldn't very well let the crown sit in lost and found forever, could I?"

"Right, you didn't steal it; it was your payment for rescuing them all from the pirates," Stephan teased.

I liked that explanation better. "Yes, payment, that's right."

"Well, we better get you an even better dress if that's the case. Nothing you own will live up to the requirements of royalty," Stephan said. "We'll have to go to one of the bigger cities like Edinburgh or something and find a seamstress to make you a custom dress."

"Weren't you planning on taking her to Edinburgh in a couple of days anyway?" Forrest asked.

Stephan nodded.

"I need to use the bathroom," I said, and nudged Forrest's leg. "Let me out."

Forrest slid out of the booth to let me out.

As I walked back out of the bathroom, a woman who was walking in asked, "So, which of those men is yours?"

She had an American accent, so I assumed she was a

tourist as well.

I smiled sweetly as I replied, "All of them."

She blinked. "What?"

"All of those men are mine. I'm married to all of them."

Her mouth dropped. "You're being serious?"

I nodded. "Yep."

"How many wives do they have?" she asked, smirking a bit.

I held up one finger and pointed it at myself. "Me and only me. I'm all the woman they need." With a wink, I strutted away from her and back to the table.

Forrest stood so I could sit and kissed my cheek as I did. "What's got you smiling so much?"

"Oh, I'm just making waves, is all."

"Oh no," Dane whispered. "That sounds incredibly ominous."

Laughing, I shook my head. "A woman just asked which of you was mine, and I explained you were all mine."

"You are a spoiled woman," Dane said.

I beamed. "Fuck yes, I am."

I really, truly was spoiled.

"Don't worry, I won't let it go to my head," I swore and took a drink of my beer.

"Too late," Arcadio whispered.

I kicked him under the table and glared.

He winced. "I was joking."

Forrest and Dane laughed.

"So, what's the plan for tomorrow?" I asked as I relaxed back into the booth, squished deliciously between Dane and Forrest.

"Relaxation," Stephan answered. "Tomorrow, we have no plans except to relax around the new property and enjoy our time together."

"And try to get Paige to say dada," Arcadio added.

"So, I get to sleep in?" I asked.

"Only if you share my bed tonight," Forrest murmured in my ear in a low voice.

I shivered. "Bribery will get you very far, good sir," I smirked. "I suppose I could share your bed. Shea did keep me really warm last night, though. Hopefully, you'll be able to keep me just as warm, or I may run off to his room."

Forrest set his hand on my thigh and squeezed. "Trust me, you won't be able to run off in the middle of the night or the next day once I'm done with you."

Dane and Arcadio snickered while Stephan smirked.

"Promises, promises," I taunted Forrest.

He smiled, leaned down, and with his lips just a breath away from mine, whispered, "You'll just have to wait and see, *Baroness.*"

I tried to kiss him, but he leaned back and started drinking more of his beer with a satisfied smile.

Oh, I was so going to get him back later for that tease.

"Did you know that there is a horse stable not too far from the castle, where you can schedule riding lessons or rent horses to ride around our land or the beach?" Stephan asked me.

My mouth dropped. "Really?"

He nodded. "While the castle does have some land, I wouldn't recommend building a barn and trying to keep horses there, but we could lease a horse for you if you wanted to do more than rent one for an afternoon."

"Would you go riding with me?" I asked hopefully.

"Of course," he replied immediately. "It's been a long time since I've ridden, but I loved to do it when I was younger."

Picturing him in riding breeches on a horse was doing all kinds of things to my body.

"I'm surprised we aren't being forced to attend parties with some of your rich friends," I commented to Stephan. "Don't you normally attend a bunch of functions and things while you're traveling?"

"I used to attend a lot of functions to keep up appearances, ensure the paparazzi saw me taking women back to my hotel rooms, and keep my name in the papers to stay relevant and help my stock prices." He looked at the table, frowning a bit, deep in thought. "I hadn't really thought about it since I was mostly coming here for you, but I suppose we should make an appearance or two."

Shit! That had totally backfired on me. I didn't *want* to go to any events. I'd just meant to get him talking about ones he had been to.

"Oh, I don't think we need to go to anything. Now that you're married, you can just explain I've made you boring." A nervous chuckle left me that I could tell all of the men saw right through.

Stephan looked up with a wicked gleam in his eyes and a huge smile. "My wife, boring? Please, I'd hazard to say you're the most interesting woman on this continent. In fact, I guarantee anyone would throw open their doors to welcome you in. Yes, we definitely need to find some events to go to."

"Already on it," Dane answered with his head bent over his phone.

Draining the rest of my drink, I looked up at Forrest. "Refill, please."

"I'll get them," Stephan said and stood.

Once he walked away, Dane leaned over and said, "He's worried about you."

69

"Me?" I asked and looked at Stephan chatting with the pretty bartender and then back at Dane. "Why?"

"He thinks you're going to run away if he doesn't acclimate you to the whole celebrity thing. He wants to take you to more functions so there's good press of you attending–without being accosted again–and show you that these things can be fun."

"It wasn't his fault those bitches pushed me, and I know they didn't intend to push me over the edge; I tripped on my dress." Not that they'd likely have shed a tear if I had died and left Stephan single again.

"He wants to spoil you but feels like he keeps doing things that are keeping you at home, and he wants to make sure you know he isn't ashamed of you and wants you to go out in public with him. So, do us all a favor and whine a bit like you do, but please go to some functions with him and have a good time, okay? He's going to wear a moat in his room from all the pacing he's doing trying to figure out ways to make you happier," Dane said.

Make me happier? How could that be his priority? I was happier now than I had ever been in my life. Spoiled. Loved. Ecstatic.

Stephan picked up the tray, and I glared at the bartender as she set her hand on his atop it. She was getting dangerously close to pissing me off.

"Understood," I replied to Dane while continuing to glare at the woman.

Stephan turned and looked at me. His lip twitched a bit before he relaxed into a neutral expression. He set the drinks down for us and sat in his seat.

"Something funny?" I asked as I picked up my drink.

"You're incredibly beautiful when you're jealous," he

answered. A sweet smile tilted his lips up just a bit, but amusement shone in his eyes.

"She's going to lose her hand if she's not careful," I muttered and took a drink.

No one laughed. Probably because they knew I was only partially kidding.

"No maiming," Stephan ordered me, still smiling and amused.

"No promises," I said and smiled back.

Arcadio chuckled.

"Alright, I've scheduled you for three functions, including one where you'll get to meet royalty," Dane said.

"Royalty?" I screeched.

He nodded. "Actually, we'll all be there, kids included."

"Oh, the kids get to meet their first royals. How cute." I squealed, imagining the cute pictures I would show off to my friends.

A group of guys staggered out the door, and I looked behind us to see who was left in the bar. Noticing the darts were now open, I asked, "Who wants to lose at darts tonight?"

"Oh, you're on," Dane replied immediately.

"Count me in," Forrest said and stood.

"I'll stay here and watch from a safe distance," Stephan answered when I looked at him.

"We've only had two drinks." I rolled my eyes but kissed his cheek before following after Forrest and Dane, who had already taken all the darts off the board where the last group had left them.

"I'll stay with Stephan," Arcadio said.

I tensed a moment. Was he more hurt than he had let on? Was he staying sitting because his foot hurt? Or was he just being responsible by keeping the weight off? Or was he just staying by Stephan, since Stephan was the boss and we really shouldn't leave him by himself so far away from us? Even though we were in the same bar, someone could come in and shoot him while we were throwing darts, and we wouldn't have enough time to react.

"He's keeping the weight off his foot so he can recover faster," Forrest whispered in my ear, making me jump and punch him in the stomach out of instinct.

He let out an "oof" and then laughed.

The fact that he knew me so well made me smile as I finished the walk to Dane. I held out my hand expectantly.

He arched a brow. "What you want? You came late, so Forrest and I get to play first."

With a shrug, I sat in the nearest chair and sipped on my drink. "Fine, I'll play the winner."

And totally ogle their two fine butts as I watched.

"What are we betting?" Dane asked Forrest when he finally made it over.

"Two hundred," Forrest replied.

"One hundred and Amelia for the night," Dane countered.

My brows rose, but I didn't argue.

Forrest crossed his arms, flexing his biceps and giving me an even better view. "Two hundred, Amelia for the night, and Wednesday night."

Wednesday night? What was Wednesday night?

Dane frowned. "No."

Forrest's eyes widened. "Okay, just the money and Amelia."

Dane's frown didn't ease, but he nodded his agreement.

Bet settled, they took up their spots and started throwing the darts at the board. Both were good at darts, much better than me, even though I tried to act like I was good. I knew my limits, and darts were where I sucked.

In order to win, I had to use underhanded tricks like flirtation and getting them drunker than I was.

"Erina and Marlee want to plan an entire girls' week," I said to distract them.

As anticipated, both turned towards me.

"A week?" Dane asked, scowling.

I nodded. "At a beach resort that they own. They were going to block it so no other guests could book a stay then. So that the three of us would have the entire resort and private beach to ourselves."

"Is Erina bringing her husbands?" Forrest asked.

Dane threw his dart a bit harder than he had a second ago.

I shrugged. "We haven't worked out all the details yet."

Dane spun to face me. "If she gets to bring one, you have to bring one of us."

"Well, I'll probably have my own guard by then," I commented. "So, you guys can stay with Stephan and continue working."

"You think we'll be able to work while you're in a different country without us?" Dane asked.

Forrest threw his dart, and I swore I heard the board crack.

My lip twitched as a smirk tried to take over, but I held it in check and cleared my throat. "Life must move on. You wouldn't have followed me a couple years ago when we were dating."

"The fuck we wouldn't have," Forrest grumbled. "We just wouldn't have let you know."

My eyes widened. "You stalked me?"

He looked at me, eyes widened, and realized his mistake. "No."

That answer had been too fast.

I stood up and glared up into his handsome face. "When?"

"When what?"

"Forrest!" I snapped.

"It was before we talked to you and asked you out," he admitted.

"Forrest!" Dane yelled and threw his dart, missing the dartboard and hitting the wall beside it.

"When you went on that trip to Portland," Forrest continued. "Dane and I followed you."

I'd told them about it during one of the few times I'd talked to them when they were customers of mine at my coffee shop. It had been a quick trip to see the sights and relax, but I'd felt like someone was following me the entire time and had been freaked out. Knowing it was them made me happy and irritated at the same time. Irritated because I might have been able to spend time with them while there and gotten to know them better. Intimately. Naked.

"Does Stephan know?" I asked, my heart beating a bit faster than it had been a second ago.

He shook his head.

Dane stepped closer. "Don't tell him. Please."

Oh, my god! I had blackmail!

"You can't be with me all the time," I reminded them. "I'm going to get a bodyguard, who isn't one of you, and you're going to have to be okay with me doing things, attending events, and leaving our territory."

"We won't ever be okay with it," Dane grumbled.

Forrest threw his dart, hitting an outer ring.

"But we will not stop you," Dane added with a sigh and rubbed his temples.

"Even if we won't sleep the entire time you're gone,"

Forrest said. "And totally won't tap into any surveillance cameras or anything."

"Definitely won't do that," Dane said with a serious expression.

I smiled. "Of course you won't."

Dane threw his next dart, hitting the bullseye.

"Are you serious about going, though? Or just trying to rile us up?" Forrest asked.

"Serious," I answered. "We're thinking about doing it at the next Mafia Weekend two years from now. This one, we already have plans for that weekend."

Forrest threw his dart, hitting the bullseye with enough force I definitely heard a crack.

"At least I'll be in the same city this year," I offered as consolation. "You can come rescue me in half an hour, tops."

Dane's dart hit the outer ring as he grumbled beneath his breath.

After a few more throws, I downed my drink and stood to play the winner, Forrest.

"So," I began, and cracked my neck side to side, "what are we betting?"

Dane went to the bar to get another drink, still grumbling and scowling.

"If I win, you have to wear a piece of jewelry with a tracker in it," he said stone-faced.

"To what?" I asked.

"Everywhere," he said.

I scoffed and shook my head. "Really?"

"I'm serious."

"Have you discussed this with Stephan?" I asked and arched a brow.

His crossed arms dropped, and his stoney expression

cracked a bit. "No."

Ha!

I wasn't opposed to wearing it, honestly. I wanted all of them to do the same.

"Fine, my bet is that you have to wear one," I countered.

His eyes widened. "What?"

"If I win, you have to wear one and then help me convince the others. You guys aren't the only ones who worry. I was going crazy tonight when you weren't answering."

His face softened, and he pulled me into a hug, his warmth engulfing me and his scent surrounding me. He smelled…so good. "I'm sorry. I didn't mean to worry you."

I gripped the back of his shirt and breathed him in a moment. "I know. You have to realize that you guys aren't the only ones who worry. I can't lose you…any of you."

They each owned a part of my soul, and losing them would mean losing that part of me. I couldn't bear it.

"I promise that I'm being safe. Before you came along, I wouldn't have even let Arcadio come with me tonight, but I know I have to let my pride simmer to focus on coming home. I don't ever want to make you cry, and I know me not coming home would definitely make you cry."

I tightened my grip on him and nodded. "It would. So many tears. So many nights of tears."

He pushed me back and smiled down at me. "Well, it's a good thing I'm being careful then."

"Right. Okay." I stepped back and shook myself. "Let's play so I can beat you for once."

"Oh, we'll see about that. I've got the others' interests at play now, too. If I lose, they'll bitch at me for weeks." He was smiling as he said it, knowing that the bitching would last maybe an hour.

"Well, you can go first if you want," I offered. "Since you are currently the champion."

He dipped his head. "How thoughtful of you, Baroness."

Our game went by quick, and somehow, I won.

"Oh yeah!" I screamed and shook my butt as I danced around Forrest in a circle. "I won. You lost. I'm the champ."

"Want to take on a real man?" a deep voice asked behind me.

I spun around and eyed the large American in cowboy boots, jeans, and a flannel button-up shirt. He had a trucker hat on with a common beer logo and a thick handlebar mustache he smoothed down with his finger and thumb as he looked at me.

"Sorry, partner, but I'm not interested."

"Not a fan of your fellow American men?" he asked, cocked his right foot on his heel, and put his thumbs in his belt loops.

He thought Forrest wasn't American?

"Ay, why don'tcha piss off? This lass is 'ere wit' me," Forrest said with a thick and sexy as sin accent.

I bit my lip and grunted.

Forrest's hand pressed into my lower back where the guy couldn't see, likely from my sound.

The man, not accepting it, smiled wide. "You ever been with a cowboy, little lady?"

Little lady? What fake-ass yuppie crap was this? I grew up around real cowboys, and they didn't say "little lady" unless they were teasing someone.

"I've been with a real cowboy a time or two," I admitted. "His boots weren't nearly as shiny as yours." I winked and turned around to look up at Forrest. "I need a drink."

"Best buy ye one then, shouldn't I?" he asked, still using that thick accent that had my lower stomach warming.

"You think I'm fake just because I cleaned my boots for this trip?" the fake cowboy asked.

I sighed and spun back around, walking right up to him. "No, it's that your boots have no wear on them, which means you bought them recently. Again, not an indicator that you're fake, but no one says 'little lady' unless they're being demeaning or playing it up for city girls. I was raised in the country."

"You?" he asked with a scoff. "You don't look like a country girl."

"Why?" I asked. "Because I've got all my teeth and I'm wearing nice clothes? You think I'm going to come out looking for men in dirty things?"

"You're just proving my point about how you felt about me," he said with a satisfied smile.

"Look, I'm sorry I was rude, but I'm obviously here with this guy, and you pissed me off. So, please beat it." I raised my left hand, showing off my ring. "I'm married."

"To this guy?" he asked with wide eyes.

"Yes," I answered and let Forrest put his arms around me.

"Sorry, man, but this one is mine," Forrest said in his normal voice.

I looked up and pouted. "Use the voice more. It's hot."

He chuckled. "Tonight, I'll use it all you want."

"Yes, please," I said, my voice breathy.

"Here," Dane said and held out a drink for me.

"This your husband, too?" the guy asked scathingly.

"Actually, yes," I answered honestly.

"Well, I thought you looked easy, but this easy wasn't what I was planning on," he said.

Before I could react, Dane and Forrest punched the asshole in the face at the same time.

"Whoops," I said and drank my beer. "You pissed them off."

"You alright?" Stephan called out from the booth where he was still sitting.

I raised my beer and winked at him. "We're good."

Two guys stood from the nearest barstools and walked towards us.

"Look, he has friends," I commented.

Dane cracked his knuckles. "Goodie, I was getting bored."

I sat back down in the chair I'd vacated and drank more of my beer. "Don't wear yourself out too much," I ordered Forrest. "You're supposed to ensure I can't walk by morning, remember?"

The four men exchanged several blows, and I continued drinking my beer.

The bartender picked up the phone, but Stephan walked to her, and she put it down quickly, distracted by his charm.

"This is sure taking you a long time. You boys out of shape?" I asked as Dane ducked a punch from one guy and punched the other in the stomach.

"It has been a while since I've been in a bar fight," Forrest admitted.

"Rusty?" I asked.

They finally knocked the three men unconscious, walked over to the table Stephan and Arcadio sat at and plopped down into the booth.

"We need to resume your training routines," Stephan said with a sad shake of his head.

I skipped over to them, a huge smile on my face. "Ox is going to tease you so bad."

"You're not telling Ox," Dane said.

I scoffed. "Of course I am. We're going to have a big laugh about it, and I'll even show him the video I recorded."

"Video?" Dane and Forrest asked.

"Actually, it was Jackal who recorded it," I admitted with a shrug of one shoulder. "But he'll give it to me, and I'll show Ox when we get home."

"Boss," Dane pleaded.

Stephan took a drink of his water, stone-faced. "Mobsterina does as she likes. You'll have to find some bribe to convince her not to show him. You'll have to bribe Jackal, too, though I doubt you'll be able to."

"Blackmail," Forrest said with a sigh. "Even the boss is allowing us to be blackmailed now."

"You brought this upon yourself," Stephan said. He looked at me. "So, what did you win for beating Forrest?"

My smile disappeared, and I pinched my lips together.

Stephan's eyes narrowed suspiciously.

"Nothing," I answered after a moment.

Forrest snickered. "He's going to find out eventually, Amelia. Just tell him."

I didn't think Stephan would actually get mad, but that didn't mean he wouldn't get upset that I'd bypassed him and essentially given Forrest an order.

My shoulders slumped forward as I sighed. "Forrest has to wear a piece of jewelry with a tracker."

Watching carefully for Stephan's reaction, I was surprised when he smiled.

"You are truly brilliant sometimes, Mobsterina." He reached across the table and patted my hand.

"You're...not mad?"

He tilted his head sideways as he looked at me. "Mad? Why on earth would I be mad?"

I fidgeted with the hem of my shirt. "Well, it was sort of an order, and I didn't clear it with you first."

He smiled wide. "Darling, you're my wife, remember? You're an equal head as well."

"But I'm married to them, too!" I countered.

"Does Erina always ask Connor for permission or approval when it comes to their business, especially if it involves her other husbands?" Stephan asked me.

Definitely not. "No," I admitted.

"Does he get mad at her?" he asked.

"Sometimes," I whispered, but it wasn't really true. Connor rarely ever got mad at Erina.

Stephan arched a brow. "Does he?"

"No," I relinquished with a sigh.

"Exactly. He may ask her to check with him beforehand on certain aspects, but he trusts her judgment and that she does those things with all of their best interests at heart. I feel the same about you. You're not one to go off and make crazy decisions on our behalf without thinking about them first and choosing the option you wholeheartedly believe is the best."

The statement had me looking at Stephan in a different light. He really trusted me that much? He really viewed me as his equal?

"Oh, you made her cry," Forrest said and put his arm around my shoulders. "We all feel the same as Stephan. We wouldn't have brought you into our lives and married you if we didn't."

After wiping my face, I smiled at them all. "I love you."

The door to the bar slammed open, and four big men walked in. The one in the center looked straight at Forrest and sneered. "There you are, mafia trash!"

CHAPTER SIX

Forrest tensed but didn't move. "You've got thirty seconds to leave, or you won't be able to walk home."

"I thought I was the one you were going to make unable to walk," I teased and looked up at him with my lower lip out in a big pout.

Dane laughed, and Stephan cracked a smile, but Arcadio and Forrest were glaring at the men in the doorway and didn't react to my joke.

The men walked into the bar, closer to us, and Forrest pulled his arm from around me. I could see Arcadio's hand reaching beneath the table, likely getting a knife.

The man who'd spoken looked down at me and frowned. "Ain't you the new baroness?"

"Rumor has it," I replied and gave him a sweet smile. "And you are?"

"He's leaving," Forrest said and stood, getting right into the guy's face. They were about the same height and build, but Forrest's arms were thicker. "Get the fuck out of here while you still can."

83

"I saw you. I know it was you," the man said.

"Gentlemen," Stephan said and stood. "Whoever it was you saw couldn't have been him since he's been with us all evening."

"Shawn, they been here all night," the bartender said.

Despite her flirting with my husbands, I could have hugged her for coming to our defense.

"Come sit and have a drink on the house," she offered.

"They paying you?" he asked her and stalked towards the bar, his fists clenched.

Oh, hell no. He was not going to hurt her.

I ran over to the bar and hopped up to sit atop it. "It seems to me, Mr. Shawn, that you're upset about something and taking it out on some innocent people. That's not very nice, you know? Why don't you let us buy you a drink, and you can relax a bit. We were on our way out anyway. I've got to get home and handle some business of my own if you know what I mean."

I gave him a huge smile, and he frowned harder.

Wow, tough crowd.

The bartender poured him a beer and slid it across to him.

I nodded at his friends. "Them, too." I aimed a smile at them. "Can't leave supportive friends out to dry."

They softened a bit, and the one on the right smiled as he walked up to the bar and accepted his beer.

The bartender slid a beer to me, and I held mine up. "You know, I realized I haven't toasted my new title. Would you three mind celebrating with me? To the new baroness!"

After a second of debate, Shawn and his three friends clinked their glasses against mine. The friends even smiled.

"The new baroness," the two friends intoned.

I drank my beer and sighed. "This beer is so tasty." I turned and looked at the bartender. "What's your name, hon?"

"Peigi MacSheòrsa," she answered.

"Thank you, Peigi, for being such a gracious host. I know you've been taking care of my husbands all night, and I appreciate your hospitality."

Her eyes widened. "Did you say husbands, as in…" She blinked a few times. "Plural?" the question was barely a whisper, and her voice seemed higher pitched than normal.

I nodded. "Yep. My other husband is at home with the babies." I smirked. "He wanted me to have a night out without worrying about them."

She continued to blink at me, her eyes wide as saucers.

"So, you have multiple husbands," Shawn says, "but do they have multiple wives?"

I shook my head vehemently. "Nope. Just me."

"Isn't that a little…isn't that a double standard?" he asked.

"It's actually something that happens from time to time on our side of the pond," I said. "My mother had up to five boyfriends at one time. I was raised by three fathers. Trust me, I know that it is not the norm for most humans around the world, but it works for us."

"What about their…needs?" one of the friends asked. His cheeks turned bright red as he asked it, and I almost laughed but held it in.

"You can ask them if you want; they'll tell you that I'm not hindering their needs in any way." I glanced over my shoulder. "Am I, boys?"

"What?" Forrest asked, looking over at us.

"Are your needs unmet having only me as a wife?"

Dane scoffed. "As if I could handle more females in my life. You're trouble enough."

I blew him a kiss. "I love you, too."

"Seriously? You're satisfied sharing her with them?" Shawn asked.

"There are always sacrifices in relationships," Arcadio answered when no one else seemed to want to respond. "She is the perfect woman and the only one who could fit in our group without driving us apart. I would trade sex with random women each night to have her beautiful face in my life a billion times over."

Sacrifices? What sacrifices?

I hadn't realized I had asked that out loud until all of my husbands raised their heads to look at me.

Maybe I was drunker than I thought.

"Stephan, can you pay the nice lady?" I asked and slid off my barstool. "I need some fresh air."

Before any of them could move, I downed my drink and stomped outside.

The air was cold and bit into my face, but I didn't care. I needed some space.

With long strides, I walked down the sidewalk away from the pub and into the center of the little town we were in. I didn't even know the name, but I didn't care. I just needed space.

"Excuse me, aren't you the new baroness?" a stranger with a mellow masculine voice asked me.

"Yeah," I answered and kept walking.

"Can you answer a few questions for me?" he asked.

Why were the sidewalks so uneven here? Was our country the only one who cared that people didn't trip?

Walking shouldn't be this hard, especially in the middle of a damn city!

"Is it true that you have your own harem?" he asked.

"Yep!" I said and made the p pop as I said it.

"And that you have no idea who the father of your two babies is?" they asked.

I spun around, but the stupid sidewalk jumped up at me, and before I could respond, I was ass over head and baring all my lady bits to the world. I hadn't worn underwear beneath the dress in hopes my husbands would take advantage of the situation while we were out, but they hadn't tried anything, much to my dismay.

Now, the world was seeing it all.

I managed to right myself, and when I did, it was to find not only one person had been following me but a handful.

"Fuck off!" Forrest yelled at them as he rushed to my aid, helped me stand, and smoothed my dress down. "You okay?" he asked me in a whisper.

Tears rushed to my cheeks, and I sniffled. "Can we go?"

He nodded, picked me up in a bridal carry, and ignored all the questions the people yelled after us.

Burying my head against his chest helped, and it wasn't long before we were in the SUV and back at the castle.

No one asked me what was wrong or what happened, but Forrest likely looped them in on the chaos that was me.

"What happened?" Shea finally asked as we walked in.

"Later," Forrest snapped and continued to carry me up the stairs to the bedrooms.

He set me on the bed to remove his shoes and undress.

I rolled over, burying my head in the pillows and exhaling harshly to try to keep the spins from becoming overwhelming.

"You need anything?"

"Time machine," I whispered and swallowed hard.

Forrest slid into the bed behind me, wrapped his large,

warm hands around my waist, and pulled me back against him. "You want to get rid of us? Are we too much?"

"Absolutely," I sniffled. "Far too much trouble for all the great sex."

He snickered and kissed the side of my neck. "Only great? I think we deserve at least an amazing or out of this world."

"Psh," I whispered. "You think very highly of yourselves."

"How bad are your spins?" he asked and rubbed my arm in long, slow strokes.

"How'd you know?" I asked and squeezed my eyes tight.

"You only exhale like that if you have the spins," he answered.

"Did that guy actually see you do something?" I asked softly.

Forrest tensed and then sighed and let his body weight press down onto me. "It would seem so. I'll have to be more careful in the future. You seemed to placate him enough that he dropped it, though."

"A baroness involved with the mafia would be highly scandalous," I said with a smirk.

"It definitely would." He pulled the top of my dress down to kiss my upper shoulder. "It would also be scandalous to find out she shared five men's beds."

Mmm. Kisses on my shoulder were nice. Warm.

Forrest's hand slid along my upper thigh, touching the bared skin. "I don't know if you're up to my promises."

I flipped over to tell him that I most definitely was up to it, but that quick movement had my stomach roiling and me running for the bathroom.

Forrest was right on my heels; his hands gathered up my hair and held it back as I threw up.

"She okay?" Stephan asked.

"Could you get her some water?" Forrest asked. "I don't want to leave her alone."

Speaking was out of the question as my stomach continued to squeeze every last drop of its contents out into the toilet before me.

Once I had a break from vomiting, I asked, "Babies?"

"They're sleeping soundly with Shea watching over them like a pit bull. He wouldn't even let Dane or Arcadio kiss them goodnight."

I smiled at that image but then was once again throwing up.

"Forrest, a moment," Stephan ordered. He set a glass of water beside me and pet my hair. "I'll bring him right back, darling. I'm only borrowing him for a second, okay?"

I nodded, grabbed the water, and sipped on it.

It felt like hours that he was gone, my legs growing colder and colder as I sat on the stone bathroom floor.

Warm arms picked me up and carried me to the bed, a fire roaring in the fireplace nearby.

"Sorry," he whispered. "I didn't think it would take that long." He rubbed my legs and wrapped his body around mine.

My shivering subsided, and I rested my head on his chest. "I fuck up?"

"No, honey, you did not fuck up," he whispered.

"Bad press?" I guessed. "The pictures from me falling over?"

Forrest sighed and squeezed me. "Yeah."

"It's okay. I figured that was going to happen."

"It is not okay," Forrest snapped.

"I had no idea that being a baroness would mean baring my ass," I said.

Forrest froze, breath held, and then he burst into a fit of laughter that had him gasping for air.

A satisfied smile split my face as I cuddled against his laughing form.

"I fucking love you, Amelia."

"I love you, too."

He tilted my chin up to look into my eyes and said, "No, you don't understand how much I love you. If Stephan tried to send you away, I would leave the mafia. I would leave him, and I would come for you. I would follow you into the pits of hell and back. You are the only one for me and will only ever be."

I took a stuttering breath at his declaration.

He cupped my face and kissed my cheek. "I mean it."

"If I wasn't a breath away from vomiting, I would ride the hell out of you," I whispered.

He chuckled softly and pulled my head back down to rest on his chest.

After a moment of silence, I asked, "Will you keep your promise about telling me the favor you owe and why we're here?"

Forrest rubbed my arms slowly, took a deep breath, and exhaled harshly. "When I was younger, I lived here for about five years, and during that time, I was part of Toupee's mafia."

I hadn't realized that he had been in a mafia before Stephan's.

"We were smuggling guns, and I was in charge of the shipment that night, with Toupee's stepson as my backup. He was a good kid, smart, and a quick draw. He just didn't know when to shut up sometimes and had a real bad temper. Dane reminds me of him, actually."

I snickered at the slight insult against Dane, knowing he

loved Dane like a brother and wasn't saying it to be mean.

"That night, some nosy guys were hanging about. They wouldn't leave even though we were saying all the right things. One of the guys said something that pissed him off, and he flipped out. Before I knew what was happening, he and I were fighting four guys. By the time I knocked one out and stabbed the second, he was dying. The bastard who killed his son had been an undercover cop, and he shot him in the chest. I tried to stop the bleeding, tried to save him, but there was nothing I could do. I killed the four, disposed of their bodies, and finished the job, but Toupee never forgave me. Stephan was here at the time, and he offered to bring me to the States with him. That's when I joined Stephan's company and helped him create the mafia."

"So, Toupee made you come back as repayment for his stepson getting himself killed?" I asked. That was stupid; there were always risks when it came to being in a mafia. He couldn't blame Forrest for what happened.

"Basically, this is punishment for not protecting him. I've got to help them with altering the routes they use. I originally set them up, so I have the best understanding of why they were set up that way. But since I've been gone so long, I need to go out and see what the routes are like now and determine if they're still viable or not. Toupee is a terrible planner and knows nothing about strategy, so he's just using me to fix his issues. The only issue is that some of these routes are used by gangs and even the cops."

"How long do you think it's going to take you to finish?"

"I need a day or two more surveillance, and I think I should have enough intel. It just depends on who will be out on those routes at the same time as us," he explained. "Maybe just a few more days, and I'll be done and have repaid him enough to leave me alone. Honestly, it's a small job and a small price to pay to get him off my back forever."

"Well, just remember to hide in the shadows. You're not used to being in the field anymore."

He pinched me softly. "Are you saying I'm out of shape? That I'm getting old?"

"Not old, just rusty," I said and turned to face him, but the spins hit me, and I groaned. "No fast movements. Got to remember not to move fast."

"Go to sleep, my little mobsterina. Tomorrow is going to be a headache of epic proportions."

———

My hangover headache was multiplied by the social media explosion over my picture, which the paparazzi had spread worldwide.

At least my ass looked good. That was the silver lining I was sticking to for the foreseeable future.

Erina and Marlee messaged me to see if they needed to bury the photographer, but I talked them off the cliff.

Talking my husbands off was another story. They were ready to go take his head.

"Stephan, order them to stand down," I begged.

Stephan's fingers were steepled beneath his chin as he scowled at the screen. "I'm tempted to go with them."

I groaned and let my head fall back against the couch. "Guys, this is not going to be the last time this happens. You know what a klutz I am."

Dane and Forrest had been on their phones and laptops the entire morning, mumbling softly to each other, too quietly for me to hear.

I was on the couch, drinking water, taking my headache medicine with a timer to ensure I didn't miss it. I was still in pain, which they all noticed. Stephan kept taking a washcloth, dipping it in cold water, and wringing it out before pressing it to my forehead.

"That feels so good," I whispered and closed my eyes.

"Next time, perhaps you shouldn't mix your beer around your liquor consumption," Stephan said.

"Beer before liquor, never been sicker," Arcadio said from the floor where he sat playing with Paige and Callen. "Liquor before beer, you're in the clear."

"Yeah, yeah, I know," I muttered. That was a rhyme I'd memorized when I was young because Randolph had said it a lot.

"I think you need some fresh air," Stephan said. "The sunlight will help your hangover."

"Is there sunlight?" I asked. We were in Scotland, after all.

"There actually is some sunlight again today. We should hurry before the weather changes." He stood and then shocked me by picking me up in his arms.

"Stephan," I gasped.

"Did you think I was weak? I train just as hard as those muscle heads," he said and winked at me.

"Have I ever told you how swoon-worthy you are?" I asked and leaned my head against his shoulder.

He chuckled. "No, but I'd love to hear it. Please, regale me with your praise."

"Seriously, I totally get how easy it was for you to play the playboy. I always found you handsome, but you are incredibly charming and sweet. I'm glad you're mine, or I would legitimately be considering contracting assassins to keep the women off you."

"So, you always liked my face, but now you like my mind as well?" He carried me effortlessly down the hallway and out the back door.

"Your mind is quite honestly my favorite part, but your butt is a nice perk," I answered.

Stephan stopped walking as he burst into laughter, and I stared at him in surprise. I couldn't remember the last time he had laughed so hard.

"Stephan!" a man yelled and jumped out of the bushes.

I yelped and drew my gun from my ankle holster.

The man held up his hands, a camera in one hand and a recorder in the other. "Whoa!"

"Shea!" I screamed.

"Easy," the man said, his accent incredibly thick. "I just came to ask Mr. Moriarty some questions. You as well, ma'am."

Shea charged out the door, grabbed the man by the jacket collar, and dragged him away.

My gun followed them until Stephan cleared his throat. Blushing, I put it away.

"I'm glad you're so quick even when hungover," Stephan commented.

"How did paparazzi get on our grounds?" I asked as he resumed walking.

"Shea's been busy with the twins and with growling and grumbling about what happened to you," Stephan answered.

Once we were at the sunflowers, he set me on the bench beside him, and I closed my eyes, enjoying the sunshine on my face.

"Did you know I almost died when I was a kid?" I asked Stephan.

"I have a feeling that you've almost died many times in

your life," he said with a hint of humor in his voice.

I leaned over to push my shoulder against his, not opening my eyes. "Rude. True, but rude."

"Tell me about it," he requested. "I enjoy hearing about your life experiences."

"I was out in the fields behind our house," I began. "It was a day like this, warm but comfortable. I wasn't paying attention to my surroundings and laid down in the field to bask in the sun. A mountain lion followed me and pounced."

Stephan's hand fell on my thigh, and I threaded my fingers through his.

"I was smart enough to curl up into a ball, protecting my throat and stomach, but the claws on those bastards are sharp as fuck. He got me several times before Randolph started yelling at him. Randolph, Lark, and Dart ran out there, no guns, just knives, and took the mountain lion on. They surrounded it, making it forget about me. Mom ran out, scooped me up, and carried me away while they distracted it. Those three men took down the mountain lion and served it to me for dinner the next night. Its pelt is on the floor of my mom's house to this day. If it weren't for them, I would have died, no doubt about it. They were all injured; the claws on that thing cut them open all over their bodies, but they never once complained. They just told me they liked their new scars, and Mom said it made them infinitely sexier. I hadn't really understood then, but I get it now. Those men, none of them my biological father, had risked their lives to save me, and those scars are reminders for my mom that they truly loved me. They truly loved her."

Stephan pulled me into his lap and hugged me, his face against my neck. "You're such a danger magnet."

"Yes, I've been told that many times over my life." I

chuckled and kissed his cheek. "It's not like I try, you know? I try to be a normal woman all the time, but life is like, 'naw, fuck that. Let's toss this crazy situation at her.' It's almost like some asshole author is writing my life just for the entertainment of her readers."

Stephan laughed softly and kissed my neck. "It does sound quite like a novel, doesn't it?"

"But is it a romance novel or a tragedy?" I asked. "That's what I'm always worried about."

He leaned back and smoothed my hair away from my face. "You've definitely got a romantic comedy going on."

"Pretty sure I'm one of those action comedies," I countered. "Like that one where the bounty hunter ends up trying to turn in his ex-wife."

Stephan laughed. "That would definitely be something that happened to you." He paused, frowned, and looked at me. "You have any bounty hunter ex-boyfriends?"

I shrugged. "I don't talk to my exes, so no idea."

He sighed and rested his forehead against my shoulder. "I feel like no matter how much I try to anticipate the craziest, most asinine thing to happen when you're around, you always manage to surprise me."

"It's part of my charm," I said and smiled wide. "So, on today's edition of Amelia Moriarty's life, she murdered a paparazzi man for sneaking onto their land."

Stephan sighed. "I'm very glad you didn't pull the trigger."

"My finger wasn't even on the trigger," I countered. "I know proper procedures. First, I see if he is a threat, and then I pull the trigger. When he about pissed his pants, I realized he likely wasn't a threat."

"It wasn't his eyes bugging out of his head?" Stephan asked with a smirk.

"No, a lot of men do that when they see a woman pull a gun on them. They think I'll be easy prey and then go, 'Oh, I fucked up,' when they see the gun."

"You ever make a man pee his pants?" Stephan asked.

I snickered. "Maybe."

"How many times?"

"Four," I answered immediately. I could recall each of them, too.

"So, my little mobsterina, what do you have planned for our business in the next few years? I know you're always looking to the future."

The fact that he asked me meant that he truly valued my opinion and brought a tear to my eye.

"Well, I would like to see us do more in the technology world, actually. No offense, but I feel like Moriarty Technologies has stagnated."

He blinked three times before responding. "You didn't see the advertisement for our new inventions?"

"New inventions?" I asked blankly. I had zero idea what he was talking about.

"I'll show you when we get back inside." He looked up at the sky. "You never know when someone is listening."

Squinting as I looked up, I wondered what there could be to listen aside from a satellite or small drone.

"Ready to go in?" he asked.

I nodded. "I think I can walk, though."

He stood and picked me up again, smiling wide. "No, let's give the paparazzi another photo to publish." He tilted his head to the right. Very discreetly, I looked in that direction and saw a photographer there.

"Your head of security is in so much trouble," I whispered and gave him a big kiss for the picture.

CHAPTER SEVEN

"It's not my fault," Shea protested.

Stephen folded his arms and glared. "Explain yourself."

"I was in charge of the twins, so I didn't take on security," Shea said. "Honestly, we need to find someone who is familiar with this property to do it."

"I already did," I said as I finished typing my message on my phone. I looked up at the scowling men and smiled. "He'll be here in an hour."

"You hired someone without asking me?" Shea asked, his brows furrowing.

"Yes, Mr. Grumpy Pants, I did. You don't know this area or the paparazzi that frequent it, and this person does. I've been doing a ton of research on it, so don't even come at me right now."

"You were group chatting with Marlee and Erina, weren't you?" Dane asked.

"I don't know what you're talking about," I said, and continued typing on my phone, telling Erina and Marlee we were busted.

"Did you break that guy's camera?" I asked Shea.

He shook his head. "Nope, I checked to make sure there were no compromising photos and then put the fear of my fist in his ass in him."

It was a very large fist, and I would be terrified to have that anywhere near my back door.

"So, he won't be coming around here any time soon," Arcadio said as he entered the room.

"Not likely," Shea agreed.

"What about the second one?" I asked.

Stephan smirked and then schooled his features into a blank mask.

Shea's eyes widened. "What?"

"There was a second one hiding in the garden who managed to take our picture before we came inside," I answered.

Shea walked out of the room with an angry frown on his face.

"He's going to stress about this the rest of the time we are here," Dane said from his place on the floor with the twins.

"Dada. Dada," Paige said and held her hands out to Dane.

Every male turned and glared while Dane scooped Paige up, spun around, and laughed joyously.

"Yes!" he yelled and hugged her tightly.

"Bullshit," Stephan scoffed.

I turned wide eyes on him. Was he trying to get her to call him dad? I hadn't even known he was participating in their journey to get Paige to call them dad.

My mouth opened, but I quickly closed it. There was no point in reminding them that when the kids were older, they would call all of them "Dad" without a care. That was my upbringing, and I was determined to have my kids react the same way.

"What's the pot up to?" Dane asked.

"That's totally just timing and unfair," Stephan mumbled.

"What?" I asked.

"It doesn't matter who was there; she just finally put the sounds together," Stephan explained. "I say we wait to see which of us—"

"Boys!" I snapped.

They all flinched and looked at me.

I stood, put my hands on my hips, and asked, "Really?"

"Sorry," they all mumbled.

Someone hit the doorbell on the front door, snapping them all out of it. It echoed throughout the house, just in case no one was nearby to hear it.

Arcadio had a dagger in his hand as he headed to the front door.

"That's probably my new security guy," I said and walked out. "You boys watch the kids, won't you?"

Stephan walked at my side to the front door. "You sure about him?"

"I'm not sure about anyone," I said and gave him a side-eye. "You're extra suspicious."

He slipped his arm around my waist. "I think if we took a vote, you would be voted most suspicious in this house."

I pouted. "And here I thought you were finally starting to trust me."

He tweaked the end of my nose with a soft smile.

At the front door stood a man with an easily forgettable face, average build, and nondescript clothes. One I would forget as soon as he walked by. "You're right; you do need better security. I just walked right up to the front door." His accent was light, which made it easy to understand him.

I smiled and held out my hand. "I'm Amelia."

He shook my hand with a firm grip. "Diarmad MacCròin."

"Stephan Moriarty," Stephan said and shook his hand.

"I'm honored to not only meet a famous celebrity but be considered to work for him," Diarmad said.

"Technically, you'll be working for her," Stephan said. "She's the one who found you and is considering hiring you."

"You said you know the layout of this place, right?" I asked Diarmad.

He nodded. "Been here many a time."

"Great," I replied. "We have had a few paparazzi make it into the gardens, and I'd like to enjoy my privacy and relaxation."

"They made it all the way to the gardens. Aye, that is a problem," he said.

"Why don't we go sit down and look at contracts and payments," I suggested.

"Now you're talking my language," Diarmad said with a smile.

We walked to the living room and found Dane, Forrest, Arcadio, and Shea waiting. Callen and Paige were sound asleep in swings very similar to the ones at home.

"Diarmad, these are my other husbands," I introduced when the testosterone levels skyrocketed, and no one spoke.

"All of them?" he asked softly.

I nodded. "Yes. Husbands, this is Diarmad, my new head of security for our castle."

"Elkmire," Diarmad said.

"Huh?" I asked as I looked at him.

"This is Elkmire. You are Amelia Moriarty of Elkmire, Baroness of Elkmire now," he explained.

"Oh," I said with a slow blink. "Elkmire. Interesting."

"Please, sit," Stephan said and indicated the single wing-back chair.

Diarmad sat, and Dane immediately spun around the tablet he had before him, so Diarmad could see it.

Diarmad picked it up, scrolled through the document that was loaded there, nodding as he went, typed in a few things, and then held it out to me.

Dane's eye twitched, but he stayed silent.

I took the tablet and looked at the amount he'd typed in. It was actually less than I had expected him to charge.

I scrolled down and signed on my signature line below his. Shea took the tablet from me to do a final review, but I ignored them. "Welcome aboard, Diarmad." I held out my hand with a wide smile.

He shook it and returned my smile. "Pleasure. Now, let's go over your property, surveillance, and security issues."

"I'll let Shea fill you in on that information," I said and stood. "I've got a date."

That got everyone's attention.

"A date?" Dane asked.

"With the bathtub," I explained, winked, and skipped out of the room.

———

Three hours of hemming and hawing proved fruitless as I tried to find an outfit to wear to meet with the local council. I was supposed to meet all of the head honchos, and I wanted to be dressed to impress.

Forrest knocked on the door before coming inside, carrying a large white rectangular box. "I thought I'd find you in this exact predicament, so I got you a present. Well, two presents, actually."

"I love presents!" I said and skipped over to the bed where he set the box.

"Don't open it yet," he ordered me. "I have to get the second one."

Folding my arms across my chest to keep from lifting the lid up just a bit for a sneak peek was the only way I was able to follow that order.

He returned two minutes later, an entire eternity, carrying a bubble-wrapped object that looked suspiciously like a rifle.

My fingers tapped impatiently on my arms as I waited for him to give me the clear to open one of them.

He set the item on the bed, and the weight made the blankets dip a little, but not enough to be a rifle.

"Okay, open the big one first," he said with a smile.

I flipped the lid off and found tissue paper inside. Carefully, I unfolded the tissue paper and gasped. "Sprinkles on a cupcake," I whispered, "this is the most beautiful dress I've ever seen."

"I'll help you put it on," he said.

Not waiting another second, I tore my clothes off.

Forrest groaned. "Maybe the dress could wait until—"

"No sex, only dress!" I said and pulled it out of the box.

He chuckled and helped me get into the dress and zipped it up.

My room had three mirrors to allow me to see my outfits easier, and right now, I was ecstatic about the addition as I spun in a slow circle to admire it. It was an emerald green, long-sleeved, patterned sequin gown with a thick satin skirt, high in the front and long in the back.

He unwrapped the item on the bed, hid it behind his back as he walked over, and then held it out in front of me. "I hope it's what you wanted. I tried to remember how you described the one you wanted."

He had gotten me a scepter!

His memory was amazing, too, because it was exactly what I wanted. A diamond on top, silver rod encrusted in jewels, and just tall enough I could use it as a cane.

I took it from him, and my eyes widened in surprise at how light it was. I spun it and then used it like a cane. "Oh Mylanta, this is absolutely perfect!" I spun around in a circle, the smile on my face only widening.

"You're absolutely perfect," he whispered in a soft and deep tone. Eyes fixed on mine in the mirror's reflection, he stepped up behind me and set his hands on my hips. "If I wasn't part of this mafia, I'd steal you away." His soft lips pressed against my cheek and then down the side of my neck. "I'd cut down all of them just to have you to myself, steal you away to a private island, and tie you up in the most delicious way."

I shivered as my body warmed at his words and lips. "They'd fight you," I whispered.

He nipped my upper shoulder, exposed in the dress, and whispered, "I'd murder them all."

"You'd try," Dane said from the doorway.

We both turned, shocked at his arrival, as we hadn't heard the door open.

"I'd win," Forrest said adamantly and slid his hands from my hips around to my stomach and slowly down the front of my dress.

I arched back against him, resting the back of my head against his chest.

Dane stepped in, shut and locked the door, and marched towards us. "I'd cripple you so that you couldn't take her away. No one will take her from me."

"Don't tear my dress," I ordered them in a far breathier tone than I'd anticipated.

Forrest unzipped my dress, hung it over the top of the mirror to his right, and resumed his hold of me from behind, with Dane advancing from in front.

Now, in only my bra and a thong, I still felt too hot.

Dane's eyes focused on me, and he licked his lips. "We've only got an hour."

"Plenty of time," I exhaled and arched my butt against Forrest, moaning when I felt his erection.

"Plenty of time," Forrest agreed and licked from my jaw to my shoulder.

A gasp escaped, and Dane immediately pulled his shirt off.

I tried to step forward to touch him, but Forrest held me in place.

Dane finally finished the walk to me and pulled my bra down, exposing my breasts, my nipples already hard from Forrest's touch and kisses. "You have the most perfect breasts in the world."

That was a damn lie, and we all knew it, but I wasn't going to call him out when he dipped his head and took one of my nipples into his mouth.

"Yes," I moaned and arched forward.

Forrest unhooked my bra, reached forward, and slid his hand into the front of my thong, rubbing a small circle around my clit. "So wet already," he whispered.

"The sooner I get one of you inside of me, the better," I

gasped. While Forrest was distracted, I reached forward and rubbed Dane through his pants. "You both have far too many clothes on."

Dane smirked. "I think that's the first time anyone has told us that we were overdressed for an event."

"Definitely the first time," Forrest agreed and increased his fingers' speed.

"Strip," I ordered just before I threw my head back onto Forrest's chest and screamed as an orgasm took me.

Dane stripped out of his pants and stepped forward so I could touch him again. "That was faster than usual."

I nodded as I stroked him. "I'm super needy today."

"Well, we better ensure you're more than taken care of," Forrest whispered. He pushed my upper back, forcing me to bend over, and then slid into me in one quick thrust.

I moaned, and Dane seized the opportunity to slide into my mouth.

With both of them using me at the same time, I orgasmed within a few strokes, tightening so hard around Forrest that he grunted and had to stop moving until I released him.

"Holy shit," he whispered and panted.

I pressed back into him while sucking harder on Dane.

"Fuck," Dane moaned, his head falling back as he buried his hand in my hair.

Forrest gripped my hips while Dane gripped my head, both moving in opposition to each other until all three of us moaned and finished simultaneously.

My knees gave out, but Forrest wrapped an arm around my waist and picked me up. "We've got to shower fast and get you dressed."

"I don't think I can do anything fast right now," I panted.

"We'll handle the washing," Dane said. "You just stand there and look pretty."

"Can do," I said and smiled wide, my body weak and satisfied.

True to their word, they washed me and even brushed and blow-dried my hair. I applied my makeup and dressed in my new gown while carrying my scepter.

Stephan walked in, adjusting the cuffs on his shirt. "I hope you're almost—"

He stopped talking when he looked up and saw me.

"I'm ready," I said, smiling wider than I ever had before as I held my scepter to my chest.

"You look amazing," he whispered as he walked to me. "Definitely befitting your baroness title."

"You realize, as my husband, that you're a baron, right?" I asked softly.

He shook his head. "You're the only one befitting a title like that." He picked my hand up and kissed the back of it. "You're absolutely stunning."

"Sweet talker," I breathed, my cheeks warm and body hot.

"We don't have time for round two," Forrest breathed in my ear. "Let's go."

Dane laced his fingers with mine as we headed down to the driveway, where a black SUV waited for us. Arcadio, Shea, Callen, and Paige were already inside, waiting for us.

"Sorry," I whispered as I climbed into the back. I would have sat with the babies but didn't want to chance them throwing up on my fancy dress.

"You look…" Shea began, but faltered and opened and closed his mouth a few times.

"Enthralling," Arcadio finished for him. "Like a succubus."

"Will you give me your soul?" I asked him as I smirked and leaned forward with my hand out towards his face.

He pressed a kiss to the inside of my palm and nodded. "Yes. Whatever you want. You can have anything."

These men were going to kill me with their sweetness.

"Let's go," Stephan ordered Forrest, "before she drags us all back into the house."

The four men chuckled, and the SUV pulled away from our castle.

The building we stopped in front of was clearly old, the architecture drool-worthy and beautiful. There were guards out front in suits, and they watched us with narrowed eyes.

"Ready to make your debut?" Stephan asked.

I nodded and gripped my scepter tight. "Ready as I'll ever be."

Dane opened Stephan's door, and Forrest opened my door, extending his hand to help me climb out of the SUV. Once down, Stephan bowed and held out his hand for me to take. He looped his arm through mine, and with my head held high, I walked up the ramp to the front doors.

The guards opened the doors without asking for identification or anything, dipping their heads respectfully as we walked by.

Once inside, I took a moment to admire the stained-glass windows and held back my squeal of excitement.

In what looked like a medieval courtroom, a group of men in suits sat on a raised dais, murmuring quietly to each other as we entered.

We stopped just before them, and Stephan took a step in front of me.

"Presenting, Amelia Moriarty of Elkmire, Baroness of

Elkmire," Stephan said, projecting his voice so that it echoed around the room.

"Welcome," one of the men in the middle said. He was the youngest looking of the group with a glint in his eyes that made me grip my scepter a bit tighter. "We have been expecting you."

I gave them my best smile. "I'm excited to be here."

"So, you are the new Baroness?" a man with wispy grey hair and furrowed brows asked. "You're a bit young, yes?"

"I'm in my thirties, sir," I answered. "If history is one to go by, there were much younger Baroness' than me."

Several of the men narrowed their eyes at my statement.

"Very true," the youngest said.

The man in the middle said something, but his accent was so thick, and he spoke so fast that I couldn't understand him. I glanced at Stephan, but it was Forrest who stepped up next to me and spoke in a completely different language. The man smiled, nodded, and replied again.

Forrest glanced down at me and smiled wide. "Yes, I am loyal to the Baroness." He spoke again in the other language, and I was fairly certain he said the same thing again.

"We have no pending business, but we do recognize you and your title," the younger man said. "Did you have any business to bring before us?"

"So long as you accept me and my title, I have no other business tonight," I replied and spun around to exit.

Once I was facing him, Callen, in Arcadio's arms, murmured, "Mama. Ma. Ma. Mama."

"Who is this?" a woman asked, her voice evenly pitched, yet it seemed to echo in the room.

"Your Highness!" the youngest man exclaimed. "We did not know you were coming tonight."

The woman in the doorway wore an exquisite 1800s style debutante ballgown in pale green with long white gloves, and she held a fan up to cover the bottom half of her face. Her brown hair was perfectly curled and hung around her shoulders to frame her angelic features, and her makeup had been applied expertly. She looked like a queen, and for some reason, I instantly disliked her.

I reprimanded myself for such a thought when I didn't even know the woman, but there was something in her bright eyes that had my hackles up. I'd forgotten that we were going to meet royalty today, too.

Beside her, a man in his late thirties with salt and pepper hair wore a tuxedo with long tails and held a golden cane as he glowered at us.

She gave me a once over and spent far too long ogling my men before sashaying her way to stand before me. "You are the new baroness?" The surprise and disgust in her voice were unmistakable.

Not deterred, I smiled, curtsied, and said, "Yes, I am. My name is Amelia Moriarty; it is a pleasure to meet you."

At the mention of my name, her eyes widened, and she looked over at Stephan. "It is you, Stephan Moriarty! I thought you looked familiar, but it has been *so* many years." She smiled, tossed her fan to the man at her side, and threw her arms around Stephan's shoulders. "I knew you would come back for me."

CHAPTER EIGHT

The room was eerily silent as we all stared at the woman hugging Stephan.

Royalty or not, she was hugging my husband and acting far too familiar with him.

Before I could open my mouth, Stephan took her arms, removed them from around his neck, and gently pushed her away. "Your Highness, it is nice to see you again. However, you are mistaken about my reasons for being here." He took a step around her to come to my side and used his hand to indicate me. "I am here with my wife."

Her eyes widened for a fraction of a second before she composed herself and smiled. "I see. I had assumed those were just foul rumors that the playboy billionaire had finally settled down."

"They aren't rumors," Stephan said. "I'm married, and we've started our family."

Her eyes immediately swung to Callen and Paige. Fury blazed in her eyes as her brows furrowed. "Children?"

"Yes," he answered.

She realized everyone was watching her, took a breath, and smiled wide. "They're beautiful." She stepped forward and reached out toward Paige. "Hello…"

Paige looked at the woman, her forehead pinched together, and then my beautiful little daughter threw up all over the royal woman.

Her screech echoed so loudly in the room that my ears rang and Paige and Callen both wailed.

Arcadio and Dane rushed the children out of the building and to the car to clean them up.

"Ah!" the woman screamed and stared at her dress in horror before glaring at me. "Your child ruined my dress!"

"I need to check on Paige," I told Stephan and hurried from the building. If that woman continued in the same tone she had just spoken in, I was likely to punch her in the face and start an international war.

Dane took my scepter, put his jacket on me, and then handed me Paige, who was still fussing.

"My poor little girl, was that obnoxious woman's perfume too much for your widdle tummy?" I asked as I bounced her gently in my arms.

Paige buried her head in the crook of my neck and sniffled softly but calmed.

"I think she sensed your hostility," Dane teased.

Without looking at him, so he couldn't see my face, I replied, "I don't know what you're talking about."

Dane and Arcadio snickered.

"I was worried you were going to bash her over the head with your scepter," Arcadio teased me.

"I would never," I gasped in fake indignation. I mean…I hadn't thought about it, but now that he had pointed it out, I totally could have done that and would remember that next time we were out and I had my scepter.

"What did Forrest say to that old man inside?" I asked. "When they were talking in another language?"

"You'll have to ask him," Dane replied. "I don't speak whatever language that was."

A small two-door car pulled up behind us, and an impossibly large man climbed out of it.

"Is the circus in town?"

I hadn't realized I had said that out loud until Arcadio and Dane snickered.

The man was at least as big as Shea, with arms as big as my body. He looked over at us, and I swallowed. One of his eyes was a milky white color, bisected by a huge scar.

"Forrest?" he asked in a clipped word.

"That way," I said and pointed towards the trees.

"I think he means our Forrest," Dane whispered.

Arcadio snickered again from beside me, where he bounced a sleeping Callen in his arms.

"What are you doing here?" Forrest asked the large man as he, Stephan, and Shea came out of the building.

"Time," the big man said.

"I'll go," Dane answered before I could ask who would go with Forrest this time.

"Nay," the big man argued. "Forrest only."

"Sorry, but he has to take at least one more," Stephan argued. "That was the deal we made."

"No room," the man said and indicated his car.

"We'll fit," Dane said, kissed my cheek, and walked over to the car.

Forrest hurried over to kiss my lips lightly. "Don't wait up, love, but we'll be home tomorrow, okay?"

"Promise?" I asked softly.

He kissed Paige's little cheek and gave me one of his panty-melting smiles. "Promise."

"Let's get home," Stephan said. "The babies need to get tucked in for their midday nap."

Where could they be going at this time of day? What was Forrest helping them do? Why did Toupee need him to come all the way out to Scotland?

I didn't like not having the answers to those questions or having to worry about them while I sat on my hands.

We drove for a little bit in silence before I asked, "So, had a fling with royalty, did you?"

Stephan chuckled. "You lasted five minutes longer than I expected you to." Turning around to face me from the front seat, he smiled and said, "I danced with her at a gala and then attended a party at her estate the following day. She tried to take me up to her room, but Shea rescued me and made up a fake emergency back at home. I flew back to the States and never saw her again."

"Clearly, you made an impression." For some reason, my stupid mouth wouldn't shut up and drop the subject despite me realizing I had no reason to be jealous. "She's beautiful."

Stephan shrugged a shoulder. "If you're into that type of woman, I suppose, but she's too..." He paused as he tried to think of the word.

"Angelic," Shea offered.

Stephan nodded. "Thank you, yes, she's too angelic for my liking."

"You don't like angelic?" I asked, frowned, and then added, "What am I then?" I knew I wasn't angelic, but...

"Demonic," Arcadio supplied.

I glared at him and asked, "Wasn't I just a succubus earlier?"

"That was earlier, and both are demonic," he said and winked.

"Well, at least I'm not covered in puke," I said with a huff.

After a beat of silence, everyone began to laugh, myself included. We laughed so loudly that we woke the babies and had to calm them down again.

"Her face was absolutely priceless," Stephan said as he faced forward and relaxed.

"Thank you, Stephan."

He turned to look at me. "Why are you thanking me?"

"You stopped her from hugging you and came to my side," I explained. "I appreciate you doing that."

He tilted his head as he looked at me, stared in silence for a beat as though absorbing what I had said. "You're welcome."

Diarmad met us in the driveway with an umbrella when we arrived at the castle. "You're quite the scandalous client, Amelia."

My brows rose. "Why do you say that?"

Taking his offered hand, I climbed out of the vehicle and let him escort me to the front door.

"Here," he handed me his phone and went back to escort the guys as they carried Paige and Callen into the house, protecting them from the rain that had started when we arrived.

Stepping into the entry, I looked down at his phone and gasped as I stared at the headline: PRINCESS JILTED AND THEN PUKED ON BY ELKMIRE BARONESS' CHILDREN.

"You love to make headlines," Arcadio teased as he looked over my shoulder.

"It wasn't like Paige did it on purpose," I argued. "And she was hardly jilted! He was already my husband. And how the hell did they get this published already? It's only been half an hour."

"The shady younger fellow you met owns the newspaper that published that article," Diarmad explained.

"I knew there was something weird about him!"

"Oh, there's more," Diarmad said, took his phone, and scrolled to another article, then another, and then another.

The other articles were similar but had more images of me and a few images of her hugging Stephan and then him pushing her away.

"She's probably pissed," I sang.

"Stop looking so smug," Shea teased as he walked by carrying the car seats with Paige and Callen sound asleep inside them.

"I'm going to get changed," I announced. "Arcadio, can you help me?"

Without waiting for their replies, I spun on my heel and headed toward my room.

"Don't worry; Stephan will run damage control on the articles to ensure things don't get out of hand. I'm sure he'll be having a talk with that weasel from the council, too." Arcadio shut the door behind him and then started unzipping my dress.

"I'm not worried about it," I assured him.

Someone knocked on the door, and then Stephan poked his head in. "Do you want to go on a horseback ride?"

"In the rain?" I asked.

He smirked. "Well, first, we need to go to the ranch to discuss leasing a couple of horses while we're here and for when we visit. I was hoping the rain might stop by the time we finished our discussions."

"I'd love to!" Holding onto Arcadio's shoulders, I climbed out of the dress and then ran to the dresser to grab jeans, a shirt, and a sweater.

"Where do you want me to put your scepter?" Arcadio asked and swung it like a baseball bat.

"Um, you can just set it on the dresser," I said as I hopped on one leg into the jeans.

"We'll get you a nice case for it that we can put in one of the front rooms," Stephan offered.

"That would be great!"

"I'm going to change," Stephan said and shut the door.

"What are you guys doing for Toupee?" I asked Arcadio once I was sure Stephan was really gone.

He put my dress on a hanger and carried it towards the closet. "I can't really answer that. You should ask Forrest."

"I haven't had much time alone with him or time to ask him since we got here."

"Ask tomorrow," he said. "It really isn't my story to tell, and there are a lot of things that I don't know. I think it would be better if you got the whole story from him."

He turned around, and I hugged him. "You know I love you, right?"

He squeezed me and kissed the top of my head. "Yes. You know I love you, right?"

I squeezed him, nodded, and then hurried out to meet Stephan.

Stephan had changed into jeans, and I paused in the hallway to admire his butt. My men really did have great assets. "Ready?" Stephan asked, turning when he heard me snicker.

I cleared my throat and nodded. "Yep."

He put his arm around my shoulders and asked, "Why

were you snickering?"

"Nothing," I said with a wide smile. "Just admiring you in your jeans."

"I'll stay with the kids while Shea drives you," Arcadio said, and waved as he headed back towards the nursery.

Stephan opened the front door, and Shea waited for us with an umbrella.

"Where to this time?" Shea asked as he walked us to the SUV.

"To the horse ranch," Stephan answered and shut my door for me.

Once we were all buckled in and on the way, I asked, "Did you have to run damage control while I changed?"

"A little bit," Stephan admitted and smiled wide. "It was worth it."

"I've already made an enemy, and I didn't even do anything." I sighed loudly. "Story of my life."

"Don't worry; her brother knows not to mess with me," Stephan said, and the bit of bite in his tone piqued my curiosity.

"So, you have a history with their family?"

He scoffed. "They have a history of trying to start media battles with me, and then I bury them."

"This seemed like it was more that weaselly guy from the council doing it this time."

Stephan nodded. "The lawyers already messaged the company, and several of the articles have been taken down or adjusted to more accurately portray the story."

We drove down a bumpy dirt road lined by fences with several beautiful horses grazing in the pastures. A few foals ran in the pastures, kicking up their little hooves as they played together.

I hadn't realized how much I missed my horses until that moment. My horse had been my best friend for five years during my adolescence, my confidante, and the one non-destructive escape from reality that I'd had.

As we drove, the pastures turned into paddocks with covered areas and three barns with windows for the horses to stick their heads out of. We drove into a circular drive and parked. Shea opted to stay in the SUV and finish up some work, but I was pretty sure he just wanted to give Stephan and me some time together, which I appreciated.

In a covered arena, five teenagers took a lesson from a stern-faced woman who stood in the center on a mounting block. The five teenagers, two girls and three boys rode Thoroughbreds in English saddles. They barely moved in the saddles as they cantered around the arena, obviously riders for some time to have such smooth seats. The horses they rode had their necks arched and perfect gaits, making me envious. My horses had never been purebreds, not that I'd cared, but I had always dreamed of owning a horse like that. One well-bred and well-trained that would make others envious of me.

The woman saw us, raised her hand, and the riders stopped their horses. "Today's lesson is complete," she told them. "Take care of your mounts properly, or I'll make you muck out every stall in the barns for a month."

My smile grew at her threat. It was nice to see a rancher who genuinely cared about the horses on her ranch.

"Stephan," she greeted as she climbed over the fence and removed her helmet. Long, straight, gray hair tumbled down, and she wiped sweat from her forehead. "It's been about a decade now, innit?" Her accent seemed to grow the more she talked.

Stephan held out his hand, and they shook. "It's nice to see you, Aoife. You haven't changed a bit."

"Oh, my knees are a bit achier, but not much changes in the equine world." She looked at me. "Aoife, and you are?"

"I'm Amelia," I said and shook her hand. "It's very nice to meet you."

"So, you're the one who was finally able to tame this stallion, heh?" she asked and winked. "Nice catch."

Stephan rolled his eyes. "Aoife, we bought the castle across the fields from here."

Her eyes widened, and she sucked in a breath. "You bought Elkmire?"

"It's hers," he said and tipped his head towards me.

She turned and smiled. "I hope you take care of her."

"Her?"

"The castle."

"You know it well?" I guessed. It would make sense if she lived here, she might have visited it.

Her gaze moved towards the ground, and a sheen of tears rolled over her eyes before she quickly blinked them away. "Once upon a time, I was engaged to the Baron of Elkmire."

I wanted to ask what happened, but clearly, it wasn't a happy ending.

"You're welcome to visit any time you would like," I offered sincerely.

She lifted her head and smiled softly. "Thank you."

"We wanted to discuss leasing some horses while we're here," Stephan explained. "Amelia grew up with horses, and it's been a long time since she's ridden, but I know she's been wanting to. I also know it's on her bucket list to ride a horse down the beach."

"I think most women have that item on their bucket list,"

Aoife said with a soft chuckle. "Let's go into my office, and we can fill out paperwork. I've got a few horses available for leasing and a few of my own that I wouldn't mind letting you two ride whenever you're in town."

We followed her into a small house and into an office with a wooden desk that was dark and had initials scratched into it everywhere.

She noticed me looking at the initials and explained, "My students carve their initials in my desk once they pass their first test." She moved aside a stack of papers and showed me the initials SM. "He passed faster than any of my other students."

"I had a great teacher," Stephan praised.

"So, what discipline are you used to?" Aoife asked me.

"Western mainly, but I did a little English to learn the basics of jumping." I hadn't been very good at it, so I'd reverted to Western.

"Which saddle do you prefer?" she asked.

"Western."

"And you, Stephan? You still prefer English?"

He nodded.

My heart thumped loudly in my chest, and I had to clench my thighs together as I pictured Stephan in tan English riding pants with knee-high black riding boots. I could sell pictures of him riding for thousands. Maybe I could start a secret paparazzi business and sell pictures of the guys?

"What are you thinking about, wife?" Stephan asked in my ear, making me squeak and jump.

"Nothing," I said far too quickly and felt my cheeks flush.

"These are your average release of liability documents, so I'll need you both to sign these," Aoife said, oblivious to the discussion we were having, which made me glad.

She pulled out another folder, took out two more forms, and slid them across to us. "These are the lease agreements with the prices. Obviously, since you won't be here that often, we'll not do a yearly one, just a month-to-month that can be renewed any time you come here."

"Is the trail still intact?" Stephan asked as he and I filled out the paperwork.

It had been at least a year since I had to fill out paperwork by hand, and I realized that the callouses I'd built up in school and throughout the years from writing with a wooden pencil every day were gone. I was getting soft.

"I need to write by hand more often," I whispered to myself.

Stephan tilted his head as he looked at me, something he did when pondering what I had said, like a dog examining a strange animal.

Explaining to him about my lack of finger callous seemed odd at the moment, so I just put my head back down and resumed filling out my information.

"Yes, the trail is still intact, but there are more gates up. No locks, so just be sure you always shut the gates after passing through them."

"Rule number one: shut the gate, or the bull will get out and gore you," I recited from memory, my voice taking on a bit of my mother's accent as I said it.

Aoife threw her head back and laughed. "Well, we don't have any bulls, but trying to catch a herd of horses is a lot more trouble now that I'm older. Glad to know that at least one of you will remember to shut the gates."

"I never left the gate open," Stephan retorted. "That was Forrest."

Aoife smiled. "You should have reminded him instead of riding off ahead."

Stephan scowled. "You always did take his side over mine."

"You knew the rules better, so it was up to you, as his senior, to help him learn."

The two went back and forth a bit more, and I wanted desperately to ask her what Forrest and Stephan had been like when they were younger, but I also didn't want to interrupt them. It was clear Stephan had high respect for Aoife and viewed her with love.

It was also clear that Aoife had a lot of love for Stephan and Forrest, which made me like her even more.

"I can bring you cash later this week," Stephan said. "I don't keep much on me."

"I know you're good for it; plus, I can just pop over to your place now that I know where you live." She winked at me before standing and heading out of the room.

We followed behind her, and once we were out of the house, Stephan laced his fingers through mine.

Holding his hand like this was still a bit surreal at times but also made my heart soar.

Aoife gave us the tour of the horse ranch, introduced us to her top stallions, a bay Thoroughbred whose withers were higher than my head, and a black Friesian who pranced around in his paddock like he knew she was showing him off to new people.

We started to walk by an outdoor paddock where a mule was by itself, but Stephan came to an abrupt halt.

"Is that...Magnus?" he asked, dropping my hand as he walked up to the gate.

The mule trotted over, ears perked high, and right before it got near the gate where Stephan stood, the ears flattened to its head, its lips pulled back, and it charged, sliding to a stop just before its chest hit the gate.

"Fuck off, ye old ass!" Aoife yelled at the mule.

The mule snorted and trotted back away from the gate to return to grazing.

"Yeah, that's Magnus alright," Stephan said, not at all unnerved that the mule had gotten so close to him.

"They have a history," Aoife explained. "Magnus only charges the gate when Stephan is there. Damnedest thing I've ever seen."

"I'm surprised something doesn't like Stephan. He's usually so loved," I admitted.

Stephan smirked. "Magnus hates me because I rode him for ten seconds before he slammed me into the fence. No one else has ever been able to ride him for that long."

"I made him muck out the stalls and feed the horses for three months after that stunt," Aoife said.

"How come you don't ride Magnus?" I asked her.

She smiled. "He was my late husband's, and I decided to let him retire when my husband died. He is completely saddle broken but would only let my husband ride him. He isn't aggressive to others when they try to mount him, just side-steps and moves away too quickly. It was too tiresome for me to work with him when I had a dozen horses running to the gates and practically begging to go out for rides. So, I let the cantankerous ass retire."

"And yet Stephan mounted the poor mule and rode him for a bit," I said and then side-eyed Stephen. "No wonder he hates you."

Stephan smiled and shrugged. "I was young and adventurous."

I would have liked to have been around him then.

Stephan seemed to read my thoughts, and as Aoife continued on with our tour, he leaned over and whispered, "I'm still adventurous. If there's some adrenaline junkie event you want to do, you just have to ask."

He was going to regret that offer within a year. There were a lot of things not on my bucket list that I wanted to do but weren't quite bucket-list worthy.

"Any horse preferences?" Aoife asked me.

"I prefer geldings because mares can be so crabby, but I'm open to a laid-back mare. I like a horse who can calmly walk down a trail but isn't opposed to galloping across a field."

Stephan snickered. "Sounds like a fantasy."

"I think I've got just the horse for you," Aoife said, shutting Stephan up.

I grinned at him and followed her to the next barn, where a beautiful sorrel Quarter Horse mare nibbled on hay in the hay net of her stall.

"This is Fancy. She's crabby, but I think you two will get along, and she'd be an ideal horse for the things you want to do while here."

I stepped forward and reached my hand out over the top of the half-stall door.

Fancy had a thick neck, broad shoulders, a deep chest, and a small head with a wide jaw. She walked over and smelled my hand, realized I had no treats, and went back to her hay net.

I patted her on the shoulder and nodded. "Okay."

"For Stephan, I'm thinking of Dancer," Aoife said and walked two stalls down.

The beautiful Arabian had a gray coat with brown, black, red, and dark gray flecks, a small head with high perked up ears, and a lithe body. The gelding nickered and walked to the stall door as soon as he saw Aoife and leaned down to get his ears scratched.

Stephan held his hand out, letting Dancer smell him, and then rubbed his ears.

"He's quick and requires a soft hand. If you get rough with him, he will fight you, and it won't end well. So, just be sure you are kind to him, and he will be kind to you." Aoife patted Dancer on the shoulder and then turned to face us. "So, what do you think? Do you want to ride them in the arena for a bit to test them out?"

I looked at Stephan hopefully, and he chuckled when he saw my face. "I don't think I can say no and disappoint my lovely wife. She looks far too excited."

"Let me show you the tack you'll be using," she said. Outside of the barn was a wash rack, a concrete pad with wooden posts on each side, a wooden rail down the middle, and rubber mats on the ground. The wash rack was also used for brushing and saddling the horses. Aoife walked past the wash rack and to a large wooden shed just outside of the barn. Inside, the walls were lined with a variety of saddles and bridles, all with a plaque etched with a number below them. On the floor were several buckets with brushes, hoof picks, and fly spray bottles.

"You can use any of the brushes and picks; they don't belong to anyone specific. As for the saddles, Stephan use number seven, and Amelia you can use number twelve."

I grabbed the western saddle and bridle she had assigned me and carried them out to the wash rack. Thankfully, the saddle she'd given me was lightweight, unlike the heavy saddles Mom had always bought, so it wasn't hard to carry it.

After putting the halter on Fancy, I brought her out of her stall to the wash rack, clipping the sides of her harness with the ropes in the rack. She nickered at Dancer as Stephan brought him over and bobbed her head.

Dancer nickered back and pranced a bit as he finished walking into the wash rack.

"Someone's got a crush," I sang and started brushing Fancy. She didn't really need brushing, but I knew horses liked it, so I gave her a good thorough brushing before starting on her hooves, picking the dirt and hay out of them.

"He is quite studly," Stephan said, his voice muffled a bit since he was on the other side of Dancer, cleaning out his hooves.

"Just like his rider," I said as I stood.

Stephan and my eyes met over the backs of the horses, and he gave me one of his breathtaking genuine smiles that went all the way to his eyes.

"Here are your helmets," Aoife said and handed us two riding helmets. "Make sure next time you wear boots, Stephan."

I smiled because I had worn some, so she didn't need to scold me.

"I'll go into town and buy some before the next time we come for a ride," Stephan promised.

"Okay, let's get you two in the arena," she said and waved towards the covered arena. "There are no classes for the next hour, so you should have the arena to yourselves."

I clucked my tongue to Fancy and gently tugged the reins I held in my hand. "Come on, pretty girl, let's go for a ride."

She followed behind me slowly, her head at my shoulder as we walked.

Aoife opened the gate for us, and once I was near the middle of the arena, I put the reins over Fancy's head, gripped the reins and the saddle horn, put my left foot in the stirrup, and jumped up, swinging my right leg over her back, and settled into the saddle.

I put my right foot in the stirrup, glad I didn't need to adjust them and sighed. It felt good to be in a saddle again.

"You're free to start riding whenever. I'm just here to observe," Aoife called out from the fence where she stood on a raised platform just outside of the arena.

Squeezing my legs gently and clucking my tongue, I asked Fancy to start walking. She obliged immediately, arching her neck as she walked around the arena. With a slight squeeze of my legs, she started trotting, and I was surprised at how smooth her gait was.

"Looking good, Amelia," Aoife called out.

"Her gait is so smooth," I praised as I rode by Aoife.

"Wait until you canter," she replied.

Looking across the arena, I sucked in a breath as I watched Stephan riding Dancer. The pair looked like they were at a show, or posing for a magazine, as they trotted around with Stephan posting, raising his hips up and sitting down in time to the horse's gait. It was easy to see how Dancer had gotten his name.

Focusing back on my own horse, I asked her to canter and again was pleased with how smooth her gait was. It was easy to match the movements, and I relaxed in the saddle as we cantered around the arena, passing Dancer and Stephan once before they started cantering as well.

After fifteen more minutes of riding, we stopped the horses, dismounted, and took them to the wash rack to untack and brush down.

"That was fun," I said.

"Yes, it was," Stephan agreed. He had already put Dancer

back and came to help me finish brushing Fancy. "You definitely look good on a horse."

I walked to Fancy's head to unclip her and said, "That's my line."

He looped his arm around my waist and hugged me against his chest. "You were practically glowing while in the arena. It's been a while since I've seen you so happy."

"Did you ever do competitions?" I asked curiously.

"Just small ones," he admitted. "When we returned to the States, I didn't have time for riding anymore and didn't want to neglect a horse, so I never got back into it. Sometimes, I wish I had."

"You really do look great in the saddle," I said. "You and Dancer looked like you were competing."

"Wait until you see me in full riding gear." He winked, kissed my cheek, took Fancy's lead line from me, and took her back to her stall.

"So, what did you think?" Aoife asked after I put the tack away.

"Fancy's perfect for me," I praised. "And Stephan and Dancer looked great together."

She nodded. "That they did."

"Ready to head home?" Stephan asked me.

I nodded and skipped over to him. "I'm hungry."

He linked our fingers together and said, "Then let's get some food."

Our phones rang, and my heart plummeted when I answered and heard Forrest whisper, "Help."

CHAPTER NINE

"They were set up," Arcadio snapped as he paced back and forth in the living room. "Our lawyers are on the phone with them and Stephan at the police station now. We pay them a lot because they are the best and will prove that they were set up."

From what we could discern so far, Forrest and Dane had been out on a task for Toupee, got jumped by a group of guys, beaten pretty badly, and then tied up and left with incriminating evidence for the cops to find.

I wanted to pay Toupee a visit, but Stephan had forbidden me from leaving the castle and ordered Arcadio to stay with me. So, the only thing I could do was sit on my hands and wait for them to handle it. I knew they were more than capable of taking care of situations like this, but not being able to help irked me.

Paige and Callen were already asleep for the night, so Arcadio and I were twiddling our thumbs, waiting for news.

"If Toupee came here and I beat him a bit, I wouldn't be breaking any rules," I suggested.

Arcadio paused his pacing, thought about it, and then exhaled and shook his head. "No, the last thing we want is Toupee in the house."

"Spoilsport," I muttered and crossed my arms over my chest.

Diarmad walked into the room with a scowl, picked up the TV remote, and turned it to a local news channel.

I opened my mouth to ask what he was doing when I saw the headline: TWO OF STEPHAN MORIARTY'S CLOSEST LINKED TO MAFIA ACTIVITY.

Well, fuck.

"It's that weaselly guy's company again, isn't it?" I asked Diarmad.

He smiled. "You learn quick. Aye."

"Stephan is going to bury that asshole for posting such blatant defamation," Arcadio said. "He just dug his professional grave."

"He has to be involved in the setup," I whispered.

"With this being posted, I expect people to approach the castle to try to get you to give a statement. I'll bring in some trustworthy guys to increase security and keep them away."

"Thank you, Diarmad," I said and sighed. "I need a drink."

"On it," Arcadio said. "I need one, too."

Once he left, Diarmad sat across from me and steepled his fingers. "Please tell me Toupee isn't your ally."

"Toupee is not my ally," I assured him. "I'd like nothing more than to string him up for the cops to find."

He nodded, exhaled a relieved breath, and said, "Good."

"You have a history with Toupee?" The way he relaxed after my confirmation definitely said he didn't like Toupee, but how deep did it run?

"He cost me my son," Diarmad said softly. "I've been trying

to get dirt on him, to take him down, but he covers his tracks too well."

"I'm sorry about your son," I said and set a hand on his shoulder. "Losing a child can't have been easy."

He stood abruptly. "I've got to get your security in order. Those vultures will be here soon."

Arcadio returned with our drinks and sat beside me. "Why'd he look sad?"

"He blames Toupee for the death of his son and asked if we were allies," I explained.

"What'd you say?"

"I answered him honestly. Toupee is not my ally."

Arcadio nodded once and then leaned back against the couch. "This trip did not turn out as I anticipated."

"What, you mean because I flashed my bits to the world, Paige puked on a princess, and now our mafia life might be merging with our public life?" I asked and snickered. "Sounds like an average week for us."

"You know, you're not wrong," he admitted.

"Somehow, I know this is all my fault."

He put his arm around me and squeezed. "It is *not* your fault."

"Chaos seems to follow me everywhere." Exhaling harshly, I stood and chugged my drink.

"If you weren't here, this would have still happened. If you'd stayed back home, you would just be freaking out and trying to book a flight to come here and help. I think this was Toupee's plan all along."

Arcadio was one hundred percent correct that if this had happened while I was back home, I would have immediately booked a flight to come here. That still didn't make me feel better.

"I'm sure Stephan is working on a plan right now and likely in contact with our allies for their help as well." Arcadio squeezed me again. "I know you don't like feeling helpless or useless, but right now, you and I are just going to have to sit around and wait."

"But," I muttered, "I hate it."

"You and me both," he said and laughed softly.

"Let's check on the babies," I said, stood, and headed towards the nursery.

Even though I knew there was nothing to do but wait, I needed to move to do something, and at least if I kept an eye on our children, I could keep myself a bit occupied.

"Oh, shit," Arcadio said behind me and stopped walking.

I turned to face him. "What's wrong?"

"Nothing," he said far too quickly and hid his phone behind his back.

I dropped my head and looked up at him. "Really?"

"It's nothing," he said. "We'll handle it."

"Arcadio," I growled. "I'll just google a ton until I find whatever it is."

He groaned. "Honestly, Erina will probably message you in a minute anyway."

He showed me his phone and the newest news headlines: MORIARTY WIFE'S AFFAIR WITH HIS CLOSEST CONFIDANTE AND SUSPECTED MAFIA MEMBER. ILLEGITIMATE CHILDREN NOT MORIARTY'S, BUT HIS BEST FRIEND'S. BARONESS OF ELKMIRE LINKED TO THE MAFIA?

I snatched the phone out of his hand and read the articles; the one discussing the kids claimed that Forrest was the father of Paige and Callen and that they had medical proof.

"The doctor wouldn't have divulged this," I said confidently.

"It had to have come from the lab the doctor used," Arcadio agreed and took his phone back.

"Unless it's unfounded, and they just know that we don't know the actual father," I muttered. Instead of possibly waking the babies up, I peeked in to make sure they were alright, which they were. I closed their door and then slid down to sit against the wall outside of the nursery. "Why?"

"Oh, there's more, but I think you've read enough," he said.

Arcadio's phone rang, and he listened, nodding several times, grunted his agreement a few times, and then finally handed me the phone.

"Hello?"

"Don't fret about the news articles," Stephan said. "Our team is already on it."

"Saying what?" I asked. "How are they going to spin the claims?

"We're going to rock the world by admitting to our actual lifestyle," he said, and I could tell he was smiling as he said it. "We're going to admit we don't know who the father is, and we don't care because we are all your husbands."

The fact that he was willing to deal with the insane public backlash that would surely come from that surprised me. Yes, there were several people who had similar relationships, but not anyone in the spotlight. Definitely not someone as influential as Stephan.

"Is Forrest okay?" I asked immediately.

"He's pissed off and ready to murder everyone on this continent," Stephan answered.

I smiled. "Sounds like Forrest. What about Dane?"

"He's in a bit of pain but doing better." His voice dropped

low, and he said, "The media are undoubtedly on their way to the castle. Diarmad and I spoke; he said he's bringing in more people to help keep you secure, but I want you to stay close to Paige and Callen. I have a feeling that Toupee isn't done."

"Let him try something," I snapped. "I'll show him why you don't mess with a woman and her family."

"If he shows up, he'll make it a public display so you can't kill him," Stephan said quickly. "Keep that in mind."

"I won't *kill* him. I might rough him up a bit...or follow him."

Stephan laughed. "I love you."

"I love you, too. Are you sure about admitting our relationship to the public? I don't really care what they're saying about me. It's your image I'm worried about."

"Darling, I am going to openly admit to everyone that the Baroness of Elkmire has stolen not only my heart but the hearts of my best friends and that we all realized it takes us all to provide an acceptable home for your heart. We couldn't very well make you choose when we all need you in our lives."

I fanned my face. "You're making me blush."

"You'll need to prepare yourself to go on some talk shows and do some television interviews," he added.

The thought of doing a live talk show was terrifying, but I would do anything to help Stephan.

"Whatever you need," I agreed. "I honestly thought you'd need me to go on some before now."

"I have been putting them off because I wanted to give you more time to get comfortable being in the spotlight. That's part of why I made you go to the gala and on the cruiseship of my choice instead of the cruise you won."

"Sneaky man," I said and clucked my tongue. "You could have just told me that."

"Ah, but where is the fun in that, my love?"

"Is there anything I can do? Do I need to enlist Marlee or Erina?"

"Nope, I've got it all under control for now. We're just going to have to wait a bit for things to calm down and then do our interviews. As long as the lawyers do what they claim they can do, we will be leaving to head home in a couple of days."

"So soon?"

I felt like I'd barely gotten to do anything or see anything.

"I'm sorry, darling. We'll plan another trip to come back here when things have cooled down," he promised.

"Well, we have a house here now, so it'll be easier." I sighed loudly. "Are you going to be coming home soon?"

"Yes, we'll be leaving here in just a few minutes. You don't need to wait for us to eat, though. Go ahead and eat."

"Okay," I said. "Stay safe."

"Always."

I handed Arcadio back his phone and dropped my head back against the wall. "Everything is about to change…again."

"Our life is ever-evolving," Arcadio said. "We are used to it."

"It's not that I expected our lives to be quiet all the time, but a little less hectic and more downtime would be nice. I know a lot of actors whose lives aren't this crazy."

Arcadio nodded. "Yeah, I think their lives are quieter, though, because they aren't living a double life like we are."

The added stress and events of the mafia life were definitely a reason we had so much going on.

"I'm sad we're cutting our trip short, but it will also be nice to be back home," I admitted. "Back with my amazing jetted tub and soft beds."

"The tubs are amazing," Arcadio agreed. "I could go for a soak in a spa right now."

"Oh, we should totally get a spa for this place!" I exclaimed and smiled wide. "I'd love to sit outside in the rain in the spa."

"Next time we visit, we'll have to make sure that's available."

"Sounds perfect."

Diarmad came around the corner, scowling. "We've got a problem."

I laughed. "We've got several problems, but I'm assuming you've got a new problem to tell us about."

"Toupee is here," he said.

Arcadio groaned. "That bastard must have people on his payroll at the police department. He probably made sure to get here before Stephan would arrive."

"What do you want me to do?" Diarmad asked.

"Is it him and his three guards?" I asked. I'd researched Toupee and found that he had three trusted men who were his guards and the ones who acted on his behalf.

Diarmad nodded.

I smiled wide.

"Fuck." Arcadio sighed.

"Diarmad, please invite Mr. Malone in. I'll go get some tea ready." I spun and headed towards the kitchen. "Arcadio, stay with the kids."

"Don't kill him!" Arcadio yelled after me as I skipped down the hallway.

"No promises!" I sang back.

After getting a tray of cookies and making the tea, I headed to the drawing room, which we hadn't used yet since it was meant to entertain guests. As expected, Diarmad was there, and Toupee had taken a seat on the couch, his arms draped across the back of it like he owned it. His three men stood behind the couch, hands clasped in front of them.

Toupee was younger than I expected, no older than sixty, pot-bellied, and had a ton of gold jewelry, including chains and rings.

He leered at me as I entered, but I kept my pleasant smile on as I set the tray down on the coffee table.

"Mr. Malone, how kind of you to grace us with your presence. I hear you are quite the businessman over here." I gave him the best smile I could and let my joy show. He had no idea my joy was from knowing I could kill him if he tried anything.

"Congratulations on your new title, Baroness," he said and took the teacup I offered him.

I smiled shyly. "My husbands love to spoil me."

He arched a brow. "So, you admit that you have more than one?"

"Well, of course, it wouldn't do to try to hide such a thing," I said and gave him my best-unconcerned expression.

"So, Forrest is one of yours?" he asked.

I sat in the highbacked chair across from him, and Diarmad came to stand behind me. "Yes, Forrest is one of my husbands."

"He owes me, you know?" he asked and glanced at Diarmad.

"He told me he was coming here to pay back an old debt," I said and nodded. "Though, I can't help but wonder what an assistant to a CEO could offer you, Mr. Malone. You're far more powerful than Forrest."

"Cut the shite," he snapped and set his cup down. "You know your husbands are mafia."

I set my cup down and folded my hands in my lap. "Sir, my

husbands are not in a mafia." Actually, we *ran* a mafia, much different than being in one, so I wasn't lying.

He blinked a couple of times. "You seem fairly certain of this."

I smiled. "Mr. Malone—"

"Toupee."

I barely held in my cringe. "Toupee, I think I would know if my husbands were involved in the mafia. We make our money in the technology industry. Stephan Moriarty is a household name worldwide, and our tech is everywhere. What need would we have for being part of a mafia?"

"You are best friends with a known mafia wife," he said.

"My friends' lives are their own, but my husbands are not them." I shrugged. "Have you never had a friend who took a wrong turn in life? I'm not going to discard her just because she fell for a man who happens to run a mafia. I love her, and she doesn't involve me in their shenanigans."

"Forrest owes me, Mrs. Moriarty, and I've come to collect," he said sternly and folded his hands in his lap.

I frowned. "That's why we are here, isn't it?" I tilted my head sideways a bit, mimicking Stephan's mannerisms. "He has been helping you with something in your business."

"He cost me my daughter," Toupee said. "Convinced her to leave, and she never returned, cut me off from her life. So, I'm here to take you from him."

Diarmad tensed but thankfully didn't move.

That was not part of what Forrest had told me. Had he withheld that from me on purpose?

I smiled sweetly. "Toupee, if I didn't know better, I would think you just threatened me."

He laughed. "You can't be this vapid, can ye? Yes, you stupid woman, I am here to kill you."

I looked up at Diarmad over the back of my chair. "Get all that?"

Diarmad nodded, his eyes never leaving Toupee's. "Yes, ma'am."

I looked back at Toupee, who was frowning and looking from me to Diarmad. Slowly, I stood and stretched my arms up over my head. "You see, Mr. Toupee, I'm not as vapid as you think. In fact, you aren't the first man to threaten me. Hell, you're not even the dozenth man who has threatened to kill me. But, as you can see, I am still alive, which should let you in on a little secret." I bent over to stare into his eyes, my fingers going to the back of my waistband where I'd slid a few of my daggers, and said, "I'm not easy to hurt."

As I stood, I threw the two daggers at his men, catching one in the eye and the other in the throat.

The third tried to pull his gun from his jacket, but the moron had put it in his pocket, and it got stuck.

Diarmad pulled his gun from its holster and shot the man in the chest.

Toupee's face paled as he stared at us.

I paced back and forth in front of the coffee table and tapped my lips. "Now, you see, I'm a bit vexed right now because I was ordered not to leave the castle to find you, which I didn't do, but I know Stephan will likely be upset if he finds out I killed you. On the other hand, I have video evidence of you threatening to kill me. Plus, if I let you go, you'll likely just bring more men to try to kill me at a future date, or worse, come after my babies. I won't allow anyone to hurt my babies. What to do? What to do?"

"I also have video surveillance of his man pulling a gun on you," Diarmad added.

"I know you came here knowing Stephan wouldn't be back

yet," I said. "I know you came here thinking I was a poor, defenseless woman. However, you're a fucking idiot if you think Forrest, or Stephan, would ever marry someone who was an airhead."

"You know they're in the mafia," he said.

I shook my head. "You're wrong. They aren't in the mafia." Since Diarmad was here, I couldn't let the truth slip about that part. The less he knew, the better for everyone involved.

"Bullshite!" Toupee yelled.

I pulled another dagger and waved it back and forth at him while smiling. "Uh, uh uh. No shouting, please. My children are sleeping, and I'd hate to have to try to put them back to sleep again."

He leaned back and relaxed. "What are you going to do then? Bore me to death with your conversation?"

"No, she was just stalling for time until I got here," Stephan answered as he came in. He walked up to me, put his arm around my waist, and kissed my cheek. "Thank you for not killing him."

I pouted. "I really wanted to. He threatened to kill me right to my face."

Stephan's eyes darkened and his grip on my waist tightened. "Did he now?"

I nodded. "Diarmad got it on video."

"Orders?" Shea asked, his voice deep and dangerous, likely pissed at hearing Toupee had threatened me.

"Easy, Shea. Toupee and I just need to have a chat," Stephan said. "Diarmad, would you take my lovely wife and escort her to my room? Shea will stay with me while we talk to Mr. Malone."

I groaned. "You're cruel, husband. So cruel."

"I'll buy you that two-seater car you've been eyeing when we return home," he promised.

My mouth dropped, my eyes widened, and I squealed. "And let me drive it out around town?"

"As long as one of us is with you, yes," he swore.

I jumped up and down and kissed him on the lips. "You spoil me." I slid the dagger into my pocket and wiggled my fingers in a wave at Toupee. "Bye, Mr. Malone. Sadly, I don't think we'll be meeting again."

Diarmad waited for me outside the room, but I paused by Shea.

"Behave, sir," I ordered him, watching his eyes focused on Toupee.

He looked down at me, brushed a strand of hair behind my ear, and said, "Straight to Stephan's room, you hear me?"

I jumped up and kissed his cheek. "Maybe add an extra stab or two for me, 'kay?"

He smirked. "Anything for you, kitten."

Diarmad and I walked down the hallway in silence, and I waited until we were almost to Stephan's door before apologizing. "Sorry, you had to shoot that man, but I appreciate you protecting me."

"Your apology is not necessary but appreciated. I almost shot Toupee instead of that man but didn't want to risk you getting hurt. Also, you're quite terrifying."

I laughed and patted his shoulder. "Thank you."

We arrived at Stephan's room, and I sat on the loveseat inside. "You'll be getting a bonus," I advised him. "We don't consider this type of thing a normal occurrence, and I'm certain after seeing the surveillance that my husbands will want to compensate you for protecting me."

"I was just doing my job," he said with a shrug of his shoulder.

I shook my head. "You could have taken your revenge but instead protected me. Don't worry, Toupee won't be making it off this property alive."

"How will that be handled?"

I waved my hand dismissively. "My husbands will handle it. As I said to Toupee, I've been threatened before, and they didn't live either. We aren't a very forgiving group."

"Noted," Diarmad muttered.

I smiled softly. "We are a loyal group and look out for our own. So, again, thank you."

"I'll thank your husbands when that bastard is dead," Diarmad said.

"Now that your revenge will be complete, do you have plans for your future?" I asked and gave him my sweetest smile. "I'm actually looking for a bodyguard."

CHAPTER TEN

Forrest and Dane were cleared, and all charges dropped, thanks to evidence brought forward to prove their innocence.

Despite my pouting, Diarmad turned me down on becoming my bodyguard, saying he'd had enough excitement for his lifetime and would rather stay on as security for Elkmire Castle instead.

Stephan agreed to that and, as I had expected, gave Diarmad a very nice bonus for protecting me from Toupee's bodyguards.

We packed our things and returned home, but surprisingly my mother and her two husbands had left, returning to her small-town home before we arrived.

Marlee and Erina burst into our home the weekend after we arrived, demanding their souvenirs and every juicy tidbit they could get out of me, which took several hours and two pitchers of margaritas.

The news was still posting new articles each week about our relationship, but we have been ignoring them so far. According to Stephan, he had a media expert who was scheduling interviews for us for the future and keeping tabs on everything.

When we finally returned to work, I had to put Paige and Callen in the onsite daycare. The staff was overjoyed that we were dropping them off and swore to take the best care of them, better than even their own children.

I had to drag Stephan away and order the others not to come down and interfere with the staff.

"They're going to be fine," I assured him. "Being around other kids will be good for them, and we can run right downstairs if we need to."

"I've already got the security footage up," Dane said from his desk as we walked towards Stephan's office.

Stephan nodded. "Send Shea if anything remotely strange happens."

Shea waved his tablet. "Already on it, Boss."

Stephan held open his office door and waited for me to walk in before plopping down into his seat. "It's strange to be back."

I nodded and sat on the edge of his desk, keeping my knees together since I was wearing a shorter pencil skirt. "Being gone for so long makes coming back feel surreal."

"We should take more vacations," he said. "It's good for us." He tugged on some of my hair. "Even in that rainy climate, you managed to get a tan and some sunlights in your hair."

"That's just because I'd been indoors for so many months here." I stretched my hands over my head and squealed. "What do you need me to do? You've probably got a lot on your plate that I could help with."

"You being here for me to talk to is enough." He unlocked his computer and began sorting through his emails.

My mouth dropped open when I saw the total. "Four hundred unread emails!"

"That's just from today," he muttered.

"Why don't you make Dane or Forrest sort through them first?"

"I do."

Cringing, I turned so I could read them easier. "Most of these you don't even need to be cc'd on. You have weekly meetings with these chiefs who provide you these updates then."

"I actually requested to be on these because there have been times that they try to make decisions without coming to me first."

"You're such a control freak," I accused and slid off his desk. "Well, if you don't need me here, I'll go work on my project."

"How's it coming?" he asked.

I shook my head. "No way, boss man. I am not giving you any information until it's ready to view. You'll try to snatch control away from me before I've even had a chance to do anything with it."

"How much longer until you reveal it to me? The guys keep teasing me since they've all helped."

His face was neutral, but I detected a hint of jealousy in his voice.

"Soon, my love, soon you will see it."

His brows furrowed.

"Tomorrow, if your calendar is open, I'll present the prototype. How does that sound?"

His eyes widened. "Prototype?"

I winked and sashayed out of his office. "Love you!"

"Love you, too," he called back.

After closing the doors behind me, I sashayed, over exaggeratedly, to Dane and Forrest's desks. "Hello, you two sexy beasts."

"What do you want?" Dane asked while Forrest sat back and smiled at me.

"I need to get on Mr. Moriarty's calendar," I explained. "Tomorrow for a thirty-minute meeting at the very least, an hour if possible."

"He's booked solid tomorrow," Forrest said.

I bent forward, leaned my elbows on his desk, and gave him a perfect view of my cleavage. "Are you sure there's nothing you can do to sneak me in?"

He let his gaze drop to my breasts and licked his lips. "I could be persuaded."

"I scheduled you for the lunch hour, and we can order food in to eat while you present your prototype," Dane said, giving me a calculating look.

I jumped up, walked around, and sat sideways in his lap. "You're the best!" I kissed him on the lips, and he squeezed my leg where his hand had fallen.

"It's actually lunchtime now," Forrest said. "How about I take you out?"

I stood and walked around Dane's chair to stand behind Forrest. "You're going to take me out to lunch?"

He tilted his chin up so he could look up at me over the back of his chair. "Yep."

"You sure that's okay? With all the media chaos going on?" I'd meant it to come out as a normal question, but my voice was quiet, weak.

Forrest spun his chair, trapping me between his legs, and set his hands on the outside of my thighs. "That's exactly why it's a good idea. Let them see you out with us on dates. We are not hiding our relationship."

"Okay," I agreed. "But we have to go somewhere close."

"We can go to that new sandwich place that just opened," he suggested and stood.

"Text me where you go, so I can send you an order," Dane said as he began typing on the computer.

I kissed his cheek before letting Forrest take my hand and lead me to the elevator.

Arcadio rounded the corner, opened his mouth, and Forrest hit the close door button before he could say anything.

Immediately, we had a text from Arcadio with one word: Rude.

I laughed and hugged Forrest. "You sure you're okay?" He'd gotten beat up pretty bad by Toupee's guys.

Forrest wrapped an arm around me and squeezed me against him. "Yes, honey. I'm back to being perfect."

Smirking, I asked, "Perfect? Did I miss that timeline?"

He pinched my side and bent down to kiss the tip of my nose. "Ha. Ha."

Resting my hand against his cheek, I kept him bent down. "You broke your promise. You owe me."

He rested his forehead against mine and took a deep breath. "I know. I'm sorry; I'll find some way to make it up to you."

The elevator doors opened, and he linked our hands together. Outside, we walked to the crosswalk, waiting for the lights to change, and I realized we were headed to what used to be my café. Sadness pressed down upon me, and I exhaled harshly.

"We can go somewhere else," Forrest offered as he looked down at me.

I smiled up at him. "No, it's okay. I just have to remind myself that although I failed on that venture, it was the place where I met you and has good memories."

He didn't seem like he believed me; his hand tightened around mine, and he scowled, but when the light changed, we continued across the street and to the restaurant.

We managed to find an open table with two chairs and sat down, looking over the menu. It was a sandwich place, but it had macaroni and cheese and several other delicious dishes like garlic tater tots. Forrest took pictures of the menu and sent them to the group chat so everyone could send us their orders, which we would place after we finished eating.

"BLT for me," I said. "With mac and cheese on the side."

"Iced tea to drink?" he asked.

I nodded and smiled up at him. "Yes, please."

He walked to the register and placed our order. The cashier was a cute blonde woman, and she batted her eyelashes and flushed as she talked to him.

Me, too, girl, me too.

He took the metal stand with our order number on it and our two plastic cups over to the table.

"She's cute," I said with a smirk.

Forrest rolled his eyes and walked over to the soda machine to get our drinks.

Three years ago, I'd been convinced I would be alone forever. That all the good men were taken, and I would be lucky to get someone even just slightly better than my ex.

Three years ago, I never would have believed that my life would be this good.

"Tomorrow night, do you have plans?" Forrest asked as he sat back down and slid my drink to me.

"Nope," I said, letting the p pop.

"Well, you do now. We're going to go on a date," he announced and smiled wide.

"Where to?" I asked as I sipped on my iced tea. It had a little bit of a fruity flavor that I couldn't place, but it was delicious. "I definitely need to take a refill of this when we leave."

His smile widened as I got sidetracked with the drink. "We're going dancing," he answered.

"Dancing?" I asked with a frown. "Really?"

"Actually, everyone is going. There's a new club opening, and they invited us and gave us a booth. Stephan thought it would be a good place to show off our relationship, and I figured it would be a good place to get you on the dance floor."

"Oh, does this mean I get to wear a short club dress?" I had one that I'd been saving, and this would be a perfect opportunity to wear it.

His eyes darkened, and his leg slid along mine under the table. "Yes, please."

"Who is going to watch the kids?" If we were all going, we needed a babysitter, and my mom had left.

"Erina asked to babysit because she's trying to convince them to have kids. Stephan agreed, so long as they babysat at our house."

"I'm surprised he's okay letting them come to our house while we're gone," I admitted. Yes, we were allies, and Erina was my best friend, but they were still a rival mafia, and it was our safe space. The only other times they were in our house, we were home with them.

Forrest shrugged one shoulder and leaned back in his

155

chair. "There's not much they can find at the house. Our meeting room is secret, and they don't know the passwords to get into it. Plus, we'll have surveillance, and if any of the cameras are tampered with, it sends an immediate alert to our phones. I don't think Gregori is stupid enough to ruin our alliance and his wife's friendship just to find some dirt or secrets."

"Erina would kick their butts if they messed up our alliance," I agreed with a nod.

"Are you really ready to show your prototype to Stephan tomorrow?"

I'd shown them what I was working on in the very early stages, but the team had worked hard on it while we were in Scotland and had surprised me with the prototype way ahead of schedule.

"Yep. My team is amazing and are definitely going to get bonuses." And I couldn't wait to show them what I'd come up with. Nervousness made my smile wilt. "I am worried what Stephan will say, though, when he sees it. It's unlike anything else his company makes."

"Our," Forrest corrected me.

"Huh?" I asked.

"Our company. You're a shareholder and his wife, so it's not his company."

He was right, but I didn't feel like I had contributed enough to say that, especially not without something of mine being out for sale. Dane, Shea, Arcadio, and Forrest all had an invention that was part of the Moriarty lineup.

Tomorrow, I would prove that I could help, too.

"You know that you don't have to work, right? We wouldn't care if you stayed at home and took care of the kids."

"I don't like to *not* work," I admitted. "I know taking care of the kids is important, but I feel like I can do so much more for the business if I am here and working on my projects or assisting Stephan with at least keeping him less stressed while he does his work. Maybe I'm too full of myself. Maybe I think too highly of my talks with Stephan. I just don't want to sit at home all day by myself. I'm pretty sure that's a one-way ticket to alcoholism for me."

"I'm sure that your prototype will wow us all, especially Stephan," Forrest said and reached across the table to take my hand. "I don't doubt you or your intelligence. I just wanted you to know that if you wanted a break or just relax at home, none of us would think poorly of you for that decision."

I squeezed his hand and smiled. "I appreciate you, but that's just not me."

He chuckled and sat back. "That is the exact phrase that Dane said you would say."

My brows furrowed as I scowled at him. "You all talked about this?"

He nodded. "We wanted to make sure that you knew that we were okay with you taking time off if you needed or wanted it."

Tears built, and I had to look up at the ceiling and blink rapidly to keep them from falling. "I love you."

He moved to the chair beside me and wrapped his arms around me, cocooning me in his body. "I love you, too, Amelia. I want you to be happy. To be as happy as possible."

"Did you know that I haven't had a birthday party in like a decade?" I asked softly. "I was thinking that, maybe, for my birthday this year, we could invite Marlee and Erina over and have a proper birthday party."

His body tensed around mine, and he tugged my hair to

get me to tilt my head back and look up at him. "You haven't had a birthday party since being an adult?"

I shook my head. "Nope."

"We are going to rectify that this year," he promised.

"I'd like that," I whispered.

Our food came out, and we chatted a bit about random things while we ate, just enjoying each other's company. It felt like so long ago that he would come into my coffee shop to get drinks from me.

It felt like so long ago that I flirted with this seemingly out-of-reach man, and now…he was mine.

"What are you smirking about?" Forrest asked.

"That I was able to snag you," I admitted. "That I get to take you home and can have you in my bed whenever I want."

He leaned over the table and said, "You can have me in your office when we head back if you want, too. I'll do whatever you want, wherever you want, anytime that you want."

"Yes, please," I whispered and licked my lips. I suddenly recalled my discussion with Toupee and looked at Forrest. "You said you were in Scotland to repay the debt of his stepson dying, but Toupee said he had come to kill me because you convinced his daughter to leave."

Forrest's eyes widened, and he choked on the drink, coughing for a minute before he could talk. "She left?"

I nodded. "According to Toupee, she completely cut him out of her life and disappeared."

Forrest smiled wide. "Good for her. She deserved better."

"So, you didn't know that she'd left?" I asked, feeling a weight start to lift from my shoulders.

He shook his head. "No. I talked with her a lot, gave her resources and plans on how to escape from Toupee's clutches, but when I left, she was still there. I never heard from her, so I thought she'd stayed. I'm glad she left." He frowned and asked, "Did you think I hid it from you?"

I shrugged one shoulder and looked down at my food.

He set his hand on mine on top of the table and squeezed. "Honey, I would never lie to you about something like that. If you want to know about my past, I'm more than willing to tell you every boring detail. I'm sorry. I really didn't know that she actually left him."

"I believe you." And I did. Forrest was a lot of things, but definitely not a liar.

"Let me go place the order for the others. It's about time for us to head back, or the others might come searching for us, and we have a lot of work to do before we get more fun time."

"Tease," I whispered as I watched him walk away and ate another bite of macaroni and cheese. It was *so* cheesy!

I was fairly certain I was having a cheesegasm as I gobbled up my food and moaned happily.

"Now who's the tease," he whispered in my ear as he retook his seat.

"If you tasted as good as this, I'd moan more over you."

His mouth dropped. "Rude!"

CHAPTER ELEVEN

Erina kicked us out of our own house as soon as she finished helping me get ready.

My dress, makeup, and hair were on point tonight, and I actually hoped the paparazzi took a bunch of photos since I looked so good.

Stephan had scowled at his phone most of the evening but wouldn't talk about what was wrong, just grunting and typing up a storm. I swore he'd already typed an entire novel by now.

Everyone had gotten dressed up: Stephan had a solid black suit with a deep midnight blue shirt, and for the first time I'd seen, he had the top button undone. Arcadio had a black pair of slacks, and a dark green collared shirt with his sleeves rolled up to his elbows. Dane wore his usual tan slacks and fitted short-sleeved shirt, and Shea and Forrest both wore black slacks and dark blue shirts.

My short green dress hugged my breasts and curves and was just long enough not to be indecent. I paired it with knee-high, soft black boots and a long chain that hung between my breasts.

We pulled up to the front of the club between two barricades on either side of a red carpet filled with people waiting to get in or waiting to take pictures and see others who were getting into the club.

"Just smile and wave as we walk in," Stephan said and gave me a reassuring smile, putting his phone away for the first time in hours.

Shea climbed out, walked around, and opened Stephan's door.

Stephan got out and waved as women squealed, and paparazzi called out to him.

Shea opened my door next and held out his hand so I could use it as leverage as I climbed out. He stood in front of me, blocking me from most people's view so I wouldn't flash anyone as I got out.

"Thanks," I said.

He winked at me, stepped to the side, and let Stephan take my hand.

The number of camera flashes from all of the paparazzi almost blinded me, but I kept my smile and let Stephan lead me down the carpet.

Arcadio, Forrest, Shea, and Dane walked behind us, their presence looming and comforting at the same time.

Inside, we were met by a beautiful woman in a slinky black dress. She bowed and then led us to a booth on the right side of the dance floor. The booth was roped off, and there were even large bouncers nearby, ready to fend off anyone who tried to run over to the VIP section without an invitation.

The booth we were led to was u-shaped and had a low table, giving us plenty of space and the ability to view the dancefloor as well as talk to each other. The couch that made up the booth was actually extremely comfortable but reminded me of the black couches in pornos.

Stephan sat in the very center of the booth, a habit from being the CEO and boss.

I sat on his right, and he draped an arm around my shoulders.

Dane sat on Stephan's other side, Forrest sat beside him, Arcadio sat beside me, and Shea sat on the outside of Arcadio.

I knew Shea had taken that spot so he could be the first one out of the booth and, as the largest of us, shield Stephan, and me, should an incident break out.

A tall, thin man with beautifully delicate facial features walked over, dropped to one knee, and asked, "What would you like to drink?"

"You're beautiful," I breathed.

"Thank you," he said, and tilted his head in a slight bow.

"Sorry," I whispered, "I bet that happens a lot."

He smiled softly. "More often than you could guess. Don't be embarrassed. I am glad to receive a compliment from the infamous Mrs. Moriarty."

My husbands looked at me in shock since I rarely had outbursts like that in regards to other men.

Stephan recovered first. "She'll have a margarita, no salt. I'll have a martini, dirty, with two olives."

"Whiskey on the rocks," Forrest ordered. "Blanton's, actually, since I see you have it, still on the rocks."

"Gin and tonic," Shea ordered.

"Lemon drop," Dane ordered.

"Buffalo Trace and water," Arcadio ordered.

He finished making his notes and hurried off to get our drinks.

Five sets of eyes turned on me.

I flushed and dropped my head. "Sorry. It just came out. I wasn't flirting; I was just shocked more than anything."

Stephan smirked. "We were just as shocked as you, I think."

"No flirting with other men," Shea ordered me. "Or I'll have to break their arms."

I glared at him. "How is it fair of you to break their arms if I am the one flirting? Shouldn't you punish me?"

He leaned across the table between us and smiled at me, but it was more like a baring of teeth; if he were a wolf, I'd be scared. "Your punishment would come later once I had you home."

It was suddenly very hot in the club, even in this revealing dress. I cleared my throat and sat back. "Noted."

"Great, now she's going to flirt with people just to taunt us," Dane said and rolled his eyes.

He was teasing, but I still narrowed my eyes and said, "I would never."

"Who gets to dance with her first?" Arcadio asked.

"Ro-sham-bo," Dane suggested.

"Straws," Shea countered.

"You cheat with straws," Dane accused.

"I never cheat," Shea snapped and puffed up.

"You one hundred percent cheated last time!" Forrest argued back and scooted to the edge of his seat.

"Stephan gets the first dance," I said over their shouting. "Then Arcadio."

They stopped arguing to look at me.

"Then Shea, Dane, and finally Forrest," I finished.

"Why am I last?" Forrest asked.

"Because you and I are all over the news already. We can wait to dance until the last," I said.

"That's a shit excuse," he grumbled.

"Your drinks," the waiter said and quickly set them in front of each person who had ordered.

"Thank you," I said and smiled at him, earning a glare from Shea that only made me smile wider.

"She's just taunting you now, Ox," Dane snickered. "You set yourself up for that."

"A toast," Dane said and raised his glass.

We all raised ours but waited.

"To our continued love and domination within our careers," Dane said.

"To us!" I cheered as I clinked my glass against theirs.

After a few drinks, I stood and made shooing motions at Shea and Arcadio.

"Time to dance?" Stephan asked.

I nodded. "Yep!"

He stood, removed his suit jacket, and smiled. "Let's go."

Drool was most certainly coming out of my mouth, but I didn't care.

We made our way out of the booth, and the two bouncers opened the ropes for us and dipped their heads as we walked by.

Out on the dance floor, Stephan immediately pulled me against him and started swaying his hips to the beat.

I lost myself to the beat and the feel of Stephan's hands on my hips until those warm hands disappeared.

I opened my eyes and smiled at Arcadio as he took his turn.

"You look like you're having fun," he commented, his lips brushing my ear as he pressed close against me, our bodies molded together as we danced to the slow, sultry song.

"I always have fun with you guys," I replied. "Whether we're eating, dancing, or having a shootout with a rival mafia."

"This weekend, we're totally going on a date," he whispered in my ear, his hand sliding down my back to press my lower back, bringing me closer against his body.

"Where are you going to take me to, Jackal?" I asked, my words breathier than I expected.

"O Town," he replied in a deep voice.

I threw my head back and laughed but didn't stop our dancing.

He always made me laugh.

An unfamiliar guy started to approach, but one look from my assassin had him turning around the way he'd come.

"So possessive," I whispered, set my hand on his cheek, and kissed him lightly on the lips. "I like it."

"I love everything about you," he whispered and ran his hands from my shoulders, down the sides of my body, and around my back to hug me. "Every square inch."

The scar on his face drew my eye, and I whispered, "I feel exactly the same."

Shea stepped up once the song switched and spun me away from Arcadio. The dance was slow, and my mammoth lover held me lightly as we swayed on the dance floor.

"You made them switch the song, didn't you?" I guessed and smirked up at him.

He gave me his famous blank stare. "I have no idea what you mean."

Laughing, I rested my head against his upper stomach, the highest point I could reach. "I feel like you and I are often together but not able to really spend time together."

He nodded, the movement making me look up at him. "I feel the same." He set his hand on my cheek, cupping my entire head, and bent to kiss my lips. "We need some time alone, just the two of us."

"Yes, please," I breathed.

"We need to use the calendar more so we can schedule this ahead of time, but things have just been so crazy lately that I haven't really looked at it," he admitted.

"Let's schedule something for next weekend," I suggested. "We can go out and enjoy ourselves."

It would be so much easier now that we were being open with the public about our relationship.

"I'd love that," he whispered, and kissed me until I was dizzy.

When the song changed, he pulled back, wiped my lower lip, and handed me over to Dane.

"Having fun?" he asked.

I nodded and smiled wide. "Lots. This DJ is great."

"I already saved their information so we could use them at our next event," he admitted.

Dane was such a planner, something I loved about him.

"Hey, next month, you and I should go to that restaurant with the world-famous dumplings," I suggested.

He arched a brow. "Have you been making dates with the others, too? Is that why you said next month?"

"Sorry," I giggled as I spun around to dance with my butt pressed against him. "It seems that way."

"Well, at least I know Forrest gets a date after me," he said smugly.

I rolled my eyes. "Glad you found your silver lining."

"It's not hard to find a silver lining when I'm married to you," he whispered in my ear.

I leaned my head back against his chest as we danced, and he slid his arms around my waist, holding me close against him as our bodies moved to the music.

Shea took my hand and pulled me away from Dane just as

the song ended. "There's my girl," he said and bent down to kiss me.

Our lips connected, and I wrapped my arms around his neck, letting him pick me up slightly to kiss me easier. The giant man was more than capable of supporting my weight, so I didn't bother to try to assist him.

He set me back down on my feet and slowly slid his hands down my body, his hips moving side to side as he followed his hands and dropped down while dancing.

Shea may have been a big man, but he was a graceful dancer.

Several women watched, jealousy shining in their eyes.

"You're attracting attention, per usual," I commented before pressing a quick kiss to his lips.

He danced his way back up my body and to his full height, smiling as he winked at me.

Halfway through the song, Stephan joined us, dancing behind me while Shea danced in front of me.

My eyebrows shot up into my hairline, and my mouth almost dropped open. He didn't usually dance in the first place, so I had been ecstatic he'd agreed to dance with me first. This was definitely unlike him, but I was not complaining. Not one bit.

I spun around, and he gave me one of his dazzling smiles, making my already soaked panties even wetter.

Shea didn't back off, still dancing behind me, and I knew there were definitely pictures being taken and shared online.

Hopefully, they got my good side in the pictures.

When the song ended, I patted Stephan's shoulder and said, "Bathroom."

He nodded, looked at Shea, and tilted his head towards me, telling him to go with me.

Shea rested his hand on my lower back and followed behind as I walked to the bathroom. With the large man at my back, people moved out of my way easily, giving me a direct line to the bathroom.

After using the bathroom and washing my hands, I double-checked my appearance and then headed out to the hallway where Shea waited.

He leaned against the wall with his upper back, arms crossed over his chest, and scowled at everyone. When he saw me, his scowl disappeared, and a huge smile replaced it. He pushed off the wall and held out his hand to me.

I accepted his hand and then jumped up to kiss his cheek. "I love you, murder hobo."

He cocked a brow. "Murder hobo? I'm not a hobo."

Snickering, I asked, "But you admit the murder part?"

Shrugging a shoulder, he leaned down and whispered in my ear, "I'd murder every man in this building if it would make you smile like that."

Cheesy quesadillas, this man always knew how to get my heart going.

"I would love to bring Holmes back to life so I could murder him again," he said, his jaw clenched slightly.

I set my hand on his cheek and smiled. "He's dead and can't hurt me ever again."

A man near us caught my eye, but when I turned to look at him, he scurried off into the crowd.

Had he been videotaping us or was I just seeing things?

Shea looked in the direction I was and asked, "What's wrong?"

I shook my head. "I thought someone had been videoing us or taking a picture."

He smiled and kissed the top of my head. "I bet they were

taking pictures. That was sort of the point of tonight, remember?"

Right. He was right.

"Let's go sit and drink for a bit. I need to rest," I said.

He nodded and led the way back to our booth.

Just as we were about to walk in, a beautiful man stepped out of the crowd and smiled at me.

I recognized him but was having a hard time placing from where.

"Mrs. Moriarty," he said and dipped his head.

"What do you want?" Shea asked, his words almost a growl.

"I just wanted to congratulate her on her recent title and to apologize for last time," the beautiful man said, his piercing green eyes bright with some emotion that worried me.

Last time? Where did I know him?

After a breath, it hit me. He was the man who had been flirting with me at the bar before those idiots had tried to rob everyone.

"I'm sorry, I never caught your name," I said and smiled pleasantly despite my glaring husband.

He did a half bow and said, "I am Santino Collman, most know me as Angel Eyes, but you can just call me Angel." He winked as he said the last part, and I felt my eyes widen.

He was one of the mafia bosses from the East Coast. If I remembered correctly, he was almost as rich as Stephan.

"I had no idea you were in town," I commented and stepped forward to shake his hand. "It's a pleasure to officially meet you."

He took my hand, shook it, and then pulled it up to kiss my knuckles. "The pleasure is mine, Mobsterina."

He knew my nickname? We hadn't made that public knowledge; it was supposed to be just our inside joke.

Then again, I had told it to Marlee and Erina, and knowing my friends, they'd likely told others since it wasn't like I told them to keep it a secret or said it was just an inside thing.

I gave him my warmest smile. "Do you have business here, or are you visiting?"

My question was asked politely, but the insinuation was clear: why are you in my territory for this long, and what are you doing?

"I'm simply visiting an ill friend," he said. "No business, just pleasure."

His last word was said in a deeper tone that made me shiver, the innuendo plain to hear.

"Collman," Stephan said from my left side as he joined us with Arcadio right behind him. "I didn't expect to see you here tonight." He held his hand out, wearing a pleasant smile that didn't reach his eyes.

Angel Eyes smiled and shook hands with Stephan. "It was a last-minute decision. Your beautiful wife and I ran into each other a few months ago, but I hadn't recognized her then." He looked up at Shea. "Apologies for the flirting then. I hadn't seen you with her, and had I recognized her, I wouldn't have flirted with her."

Shea didn't respond, which meant he was probably just glaring angrily at him.

"Did you have business you wanted to discuss?" Stephan asked and set a hand on my lower back, taking a step closer to my side. "We can make an appointment, as I don't want to ruin my wife's evening with business."

Something touched my right elbow, and I turned slightly

to find that all of my husbands were here now, all facing off with this one man.

"Husbands," I said and leaned a bit on Stephan, "I need to sit. These shoes are killing me after dancing for so long." Looking at Angel Eyes, I smiled demurely and said, "I need some water; if you'll excuse me?"

He nodded once, and then Dane and Forrest escorted me back to our booth while Stephan, Arcadio, and Shea finished talking to the other mafia boss. Hopefully, they weren't threatening him, just giving him a nice reminder not to start shit in our territory.

"Are you okay?" Dane asked as I scooted into the booth, being careful since the dress was so short, and rode up easily.

I nodded and took the first glass of water on the table that I saw. "He was being a gentleman, just saying hi and apologizing for flirting with me previously because he didn't know who I was then."

"When did he flirt with you?" Forrest asked.

"When Shea took me out to the movies and to the bar you guys had to rescue me from because those morons tried to rob it."

"He was there that night?" Forrest asked.

I nodded. "Shea threatened to blow his head off if he didn't move away from me, if I recall correctly."

Dane and Forrest laughed softly.

"Sounds like Ox," Forrest said.

"Now I understand why he wasn't intimidated by Shea that night," I said and shook my head. "Why do I keep running into these other bosses randomly? Can't they just stay out of our territory? We don't go into theirs without proper notice."

"I'm sure Stephan is reminding him that it's polite to request to stay in his territory, especially if he has been here for months. I'm going to have to check in with our guys to see why they didn't let us know he was here and what he has been up to since he arrived." Forrest typed away on his phone, a scowl on his face.

It was disconcerting that none of our guys had advised us he was here, especially since he was going to such public places.

Had he paid off the guys he'd seen? Did we need to do another sweep of our clan?

The guys tried to keep me out of most of the mafia stuff because they wanted me to have deniability, but it really just made me nervous not to know what was going on.

"What are you scheming?" Dane asked, his eyes locked on mine as he correctly guessed my expression.

I softened my features and smiled. "I'm not scheming anything, husband."

His eyes narrowed. "If I didn't know you so well, I would have believed that. Has Erina been teaching you to lie better?"

"You're lucky she didn't hear you say that," I said and shook my head. "She'd thank you right before smacking the back of your head."

"So, what's the plan for tomorrow?" Forrest asked me.

"Erina, Marlee, and I are going to meet up at Erina's place for our girls' day. They're going to help me vet my body-guard applicants, and we are getting pedicures." I was also going to ask Erina and Marlee how they convinced their husbands to let them be more involved in the mafia side of their lives.

"Who is doing your pedicures?" Dane asked.

"Two of Erina's husbands," I answered immediately.

"I'm coming," Forrest said.

I blinked at him. They'd all been far more trusting of Erina and Marlee since I went over to their territories at least twice a month but had not asked to join me.

"You want to go with me?" I asked. "Are you going to help give us pedicures?"

He smiled seductively, leaning closer to me so I could see him better in the dim lighting. "Yep. Wait until you see the little flowers I can paint on your toes."

"Aren't you supposed to be working tomorrow?" I asked.

"Aren't you?" he countered.

"Stephan approved this day off last month." Technically, I didn't need to request the day off, but I still did it.

"So, when does your prototype launch?" Dane asked.

I'd shown Stephan my prototype, a mirror that used advanced technology to overlay your reflection with different outfits so you could get an idea of what they'd look like on you before you purchased them, and he had been shocked into silence.

The team and I had stared at him nervously while he had just stood there in silence. He'd been dressed in his standard business suit, but the mirror showed him what he'd look like wearing a pair of board shorts and a muscle shirt.

Finally, he turned to me, smiled the largest smile I'd ever seen, and said, "This is ingenious!"

"Production starts next month, but the ad campaign is already starting this weekend," I answered Dane.

"It really is amazing," Forrest complimented. "There are so many women who will buy that."

"Not just women," Dane countered. "I know a lot of men who would want that. This will revolutionize the design industry and likely piss off some department stores who won't have people coming in to try on and buy clothes anymore."

Their words of praise made me flush, and pride seared through me.

Finally, I was helping Moriarty Technology. For so long, I'd felt like a burden to the company, but I was finally providing a new technology that would have our name spreading like wildfire for new reasons.

Maybe it would even be enough to put our relationship news on the backburner.

Not likely! The people enjoyed hearing about celebrity relationships more than anything else, which I never really understood.

"So, have people posted pictures yet?" I asked Forrest, knowing he was monitoring the situation.

He swallowed hard and said, "Worse, there's video."

I scowled. "What?"

He showed me his phone and the headline.

MORIARTY'S WIFE AND BODYGUARD ADMITTING TO MURDER?

Fuck.

CHAPTER TWELVE

Despite my best attempts to argue that I needed to stay and help put out the newest fire, Stephan sent Forrest and me on our way to Erina's place.

The man I'd seen had videotaped Shea and me talking and had gotten the part about Holmes being dead and Shea wanting to murder him again.

Stephan and Dane had been thorough in getting the Holmes incident cleaned up, so I knew there was no way for them to trace it back to us.

As of now, the only way I could see to fix this was to show surveillance from the hospital that showed I'd been grabbed by Holmes, but then we'd have to figure out a lie that never placed me at their residence.

With the tabloids discussing us possibly being murderers, I had to put my mirror reveal on hold. We didn't want it to get bad press or be buried by the other news regarding me.

"It will be okay," Forrest assured me as we drove to Erina's. "We worked out our stories already, and it'll get buried soon."

"Why are our personal and mafia lives suddenly merging?

I told you I was just a bringer of chaos." Wrapping my arms around myself, I curled up in the passenger seat of Forrest's sports car and pouted.

He shifted gears and then set his hand on my thigh. "We enjoy your chaos, and this isn't the first time someone has connected the mafia to us. There are plans and procedures, and the best thing for us to do is just continue our lives as normal, let them see that we aren't trying to hide."

"That would be easier if they hadn't also posted the pictures of you guys standing around me while I talked to Angel Eyes," I muttered. A thought occurred to me, and I turned towards Forrest. "You think he's behind this? You think he could have set us up last night with the photo op and the timing of that article release?"

"He couldn't have known you and Shea would mention murdering people," Forrest argued but scowled a moment. "But, he could have planned that picture so that an article went out trying to connect us with him being a mafia boss."

"He seemed so nice, and now I just want to punch his beautiful face," I grumbled.

Forrest laughed and patted my leg. "We'll handle it, honey. Don't worry."

"Don't worry." I scoffed. "I'm the queen of worrying."

"I thought you were the Baroness of Elkmire," Forrest teased.

I linked our hands together and squeezed. One thing I could always count on was these men doing their best to relax me and make me smile.

At the gates to Erina's mansion, the guard bent, saw me, smiled, and immediately pressed the button to open them.

"Even the guards like you," Forrest muttered as we drove

in, parking the car in front of the steps leading to the front door.

"Leave your keys in the ignition," I ordered him. "Martino will take it and park it in the garage."

He obeyed and climbed out.

I always liked watching him climb out of his car because he was so tall, and it almost made the sportscar seem like a clown car when his impossibly tall frame stood up out of it.

"Amelia!" Erina called and skipped down the steps to hug me. "I've been waiting forever!"

Forrest looked at his watch. "We're five minutes early."

She pouted. "She's usually ten minutes early."

I linked arms with her, and we headed up the steps. "For some reason, despite owning a sports car, he's determined to go the speed limit."

Erina rolled her eyes and flipped her hair over her shoulder. "Why are our men so overprotective about their cars? They won't even drive it fast until the oil is warm. You don't let my engine warm before starting it, but your car...no, we have to baby the inanimate object."

"Hey, we warm your engine up plenty," Blain yelled from the doorway. Blain was tall, as muscular as Forrest, and had a rugged jaw covered in dark stubble about as long as his shaved head. He was the best fighter among Erina's three husbands, and I knew he and Forrest had a silent rivalry.

"Afternoon, Blain," Forrest greeted and shook hands with him.

Erina and I paused, both of us looking at the men.

"They're exactly the same height," I whispered.

She bobbed her head and then said, "They actually look sort of similar, too."

We both looked at each other, smiled wide, and burst into laughter.

"I don't know what they're laughing at, but let's not ask," Blain said and patted Forrest on his upper back as they turned and walked inside.

Erina and I followed into the mansion, through the dining rooms, and out to the back patio, where I spent ninety percent of my time while visiting.

"Where's Marlee?" I asked. She usually beat me here.

"She's not able to come," Erina said with a scowl. "Some craziness is happening that she didn't want to talk about over the phone."

"Forrest," Alexi called in greeting and stood from where he'd been getting the two jetted footbaths ready for our pedicures. "Nice to have you in our home for once."

They shook hands, and Alexi had to tilt his head back to look up into Forrest's eyes.

Alexi may have been the shortest, but he was a skilled assassin, and I wondered if he and Arcadio actually fought, who would win?

"No," Forrest said as he looked at me over his shoulder

I blinked and gave him my best innocent expression. "What?"

"You're thinking about Alexi and me fighting," he said.

"Nope," I said and smiled wide. "That was not what I was thinking."

Erina pulled me to the chairs where the footbaths waited for us. "Hurry, before the water gets cold."

I slipped off my flip-flops and slid my feet into the hot water, sighing delightedly as I sat on the chair. "Perfect temperature, Alexi."

He winked at me. "I aim to please."

"What do you want to drink?" Blain asked Forrest.

"Let's go to the bar, and you can see what we have," Alexi suggested.

The three men walked away, and I turned to Erina immediately. "How do I convince them to let me be more involved in the mafia stuff?"

"Is this because of Angel Eyes?" she asked. We'd talked about the news articles, and she had assured me not to worry about it. She and Connor had dealt with similar situations, and it blew over quickly when there was no evidence.

"Partly," I admitted.

"Well, you've already proven to them that you're a valuable asset to the mafia with your driving and shooting skills," she said. "And you have helped them with planning stuff. Honestly, you just have to sort of barge into their meetings more often and assist without them realizing it."

"Do you really think this will blow over? There's so much that's happened recently that ties us to the mafia." I sighed and dropped my head back. "The articles I saw this morning called me the downfall of the Moriarty name. They're blaming me, saying I'm the mafia queen, and seduced Stephan and the others into my life of crime."

She snickered. "We *are* mafia queens."

She wasn't wrong, but...

"You're not making me feel better," I muttered.

"Girl, we've been in the mafia a long time. Trust me, this will blow over soon. There are a lot of jealous people out there who will do anything to smear Stephan's name to try to move up. It won't work. Stephan has a track record of being an honest and generous man. He opened that housing center for abused women, and they've saved hundreds of women already. The man literally pushed the Senate to pass the bill that made prostitution legal and earned the respect of millions of women around the world, not just the state. Your men got cleared in Scotland, and they proved it was the mafia there that was targeting them. It won't be a stretch to show that Angel Eyes set up the photos and that the mafia is trying to slander Stephan through you to stop him from ruining their businesses. Angel Eyes is known for his human trafficking."

"He is?" I asked, eyes wide. I really needed to study up on the other mafia leaders more.

She nodded. "Stephan is putting a stop to it as much as he can, and it is pissing off those scumbags. Connor and Brian are assisting Stephan, and that scares the others. It's been a very long time since three bosses made an alliance, let alone three incredibly powerful bosses."

"So, we're drawing attention, and the only way to handle it is to ignore it?" I asked.

She smiled and patted me on the head like one would a small child. "You're learning!"

"Your margaritas," Jasper said as he set down a tray with a pitcher and two glasses filled already, one with a salted rim and one without.

"You remembered," I squeaked as I took the margarita glass.

"Of course," he said and dipped his head.

"Can you get us some chips and salsa?" Erina requested.

"Right away, ma'am," Jasper said and hurried into the house.

Forrest returned with Blain, Alexi, and Damien around him.

Damien was Erina's other husband, a quiet man with sad eyes that only brightened when he saw Erina. His long black hair hung over one eye, but the bright blue shone through the veil of hair. He had a jaw that looked like it could cut glass and a lithe swimmer's build.

"Hi, Damien!" I called and waved. He rarely joined us out here and seemed to spend most of his time with Connor or hiding from me; I wasn't certain which.

He bobbed his head in greeting and then returned to listening to something Forrest and Alexi were arguing about.

"Probably talking about car stuff," she muttered. "They all recently purchased sports cars and have been chatting about it nonstop for three days."

I relaxed in the seat, margarita in hand, feet in warm, jetted water and closed my eyes. "Let them talk. It gives us more time to relax."

After a few minutes of relaxation, Forrest pulled one of my feet out of the footbath, dried it off, and started massaging lotion into my foot and lower leg.

"What color are you painting your toes?" Forrest asked, looking up at me from his seat on the ground.

"Dark blue," I said.

Erina pointed to the two nail polish bottles, one dark blue and one white, sitting on the table. "The white is for the designs."

Alexi sat on his knees next to Forrest and started massaging Erina's leg. "Can you do designs, or do you want me to do them?"

"I can do it," Forrest said. "You have toothpicks?"

Alexi grabbed a white plastic container from beneath Erina's chair and slid it between the two of them. "We've got all the supplies."

Jasper returned with our chips and salsa and set them on the table between us. "Anything else?"

"Nacho cheese?" I asked hopefully.

He smirked. "It's warming now."

"Forrest, we need a Jasper!" I pouted. "He's amazing."

"We have been discussing getting help for the house, more than the maids who clean," he admitted.

"Oh, I looked over your bodyguard applications," Erina said and pulled out her tablet. "There are a few good candidates I wanted to point out."

"You're letting her get a bodyguard?" Alexi whispered to Forrest.

"I don't *let* Amelia do anything. She just does it," Forrest whispered back.

Both men snickered, and I rolled my eyes at Erina. "They're like high schoolers when they're together."

She sighed dramatically. "I know."

"The events in Scotland proved that I need a bodyguard," I reminded Forrest.

He grumbled, and I swore his cheeks looked like they were pink. Was he blushing?

"We'll make sure he's ugly," Erina swore. "That way, you don't have to be worried about her trying to add him to her harem."

Forrest snapped the toothpick he'd picked up in half.

Alexi, Damien, and Blain chuckled.

Damien and Blain sat at another table a bit away from us, playing a card game. It was rare for them to stay with us.

"Is something going on you haven't told me?" I asked Erina and looked pointedly at her husbands.

She nodded. "They're worried about you."

"We're just playing cards," Blain argued.

"You never stay out here with us," I argued back. "Why are you worried about me?" I wouldn't admit it to them, but it made me happy to know they cared. We interacted occasionally, but I was just the silly friend of their girlfriend.

"We know what it's like when the media starts accusing the woman and how it can take a toll," Damien said, his voice soft and almost too quiet for me to hear. "We added guards, but we wanted to be sure we were close by if anything happened."

Anything happened?

"You think someone would try something even here?" I asked, eyes wide.

"I believe it is me they are worried about," Angel Eyes said.

Forrest was on his feet, gun drawn, in a fraction of a second.

To his credit, Angel Eyes didn't even flinch.

"Mr. Collman, I didn't realize you would be here," I said with a pleasant smile. My gaze darted to Erina, who flinched and mouthed a sorry.

He walked closer, but Forrest said, "That's close enough."

Angel Eyes put his hands in his pockets and chuckled. "I understand your reluctance to allow me close to your wife after the disaster you almost caused in Scotland."

Forrest's jaw clenched, the side turning white.

"Do you have a reason to be out here?" Erina asked him. "My friend and I are trying to relax, and as you can see, you're ruining that atmosphere."

He bowed with an arm across his chest. "My apologies, Mrs. Gregori. I was on my way out and got turned around. You have a lovely garden."

"We'll walk you out," Damien said as he and Blain stepped between Forrest and Angel Eyes.

"Stand down, Flowers," I ordered.

Forrest put his gun away and sat back on his knees, picking up the nail polish again without a word.

"You're a fast draw," Alexi commented.

"Sorry," he whispered. "I shouldn't have drawn on a guest of yours, no matter who he was."

"You're forgiven," Erina said immediately. "He wasn't supposed to come out here, so I'm surprised my men didn't draw on him too."

"Great, now I'm in the doghouse," Alexi whispered. "Thanks, Forrest."

The lighthearted banter worked to diffuse the situation, and Forrest's shoulders relaxed as he chuckled.

"You want a flower design?" Forrest asked.

"Well, your name is Flowers, isn't it? I'd expect nothing less." I winked at him, which made him roll his eyes.

"I want a flower, too," Erina said quickly.

After applying the first coat of blue polish to my toes, he took my other foot out of the water and repeated the massage and polish process.

He and Alexi moved the footbaths out of the way, both sitting cross-legged in front of us, one of our feet in their laps as they started doing the flower designs.

While their heads were down, eyes focused on our toes, I took a picture and sent it to Erina.

"Thanks," she said. "We should put that on Instagram and tag each other."

"You sure it's okay to admit knowing me?" I asked grumpily.

She shrugged. "I don't care what others say about us being friends. You're my bestie, and they can suck it."

She posted, adding a caption that said, "One of the many perks to having multiple SOs. #ReverseHaremLife

#SpoiledWomen #Besties #Relaxation." She tagged me, too.

"So, who do you think you'll pick for your bodyguard?"

After looking through her top five picks, I still wasn't sure.

"This guy would probably be the best in terms of keeping me safe," I said and showed her the ex-military man. "I don't think he'd flinch away from a gunfight and wouldn't hesitate to jump in front of me."

"This guy has tons of hand-to-hand combat," she indicated the former MMA fighter. "We actually met him a few times at matches. He's really nice and down to earth."

"You think he'd be okay taking orders?" I asked. "He seems like he might have a problem with authority. The last thing I need is one more man to argue with."

Forrest huffed but didn't look up or comment as he continued painting my big toenail.

"He didn't come across that way to me. While the ex-military wouldn't have issues taking orders from your husbands, I wonder how he would handle taking orders from you. He might not want to listen to a silly, short woman, even if she can handle a gun well."

She had a point.

"What about this guy?" I asked and showed her the page on a former MI-6 guy. "You don't think he could be a spy?"

"I assume everyone's a spy," she said and shrugged. "How do you know the former military guy isn't really part of the FBI and just trying to infiltrate your organization?"

"She's got a good point," Forrest commented and then promptly closed his mouth.

"Does the MMA guy even know how to shoot?" I asked as I went back to his page.

"Yes. He was actually a professional shooter for a bit. It's why he's at the top of my suggestions," she explained. "He can shoot, fight up close, and has a face that blends into the background, especially when you put glasses on him. He doesn't have cauliflower ear yet, either, so he won't be easily distinguishable for that. He's part of your mafia right now."

I tapped my finger on the arm of the chair as I looked over the options. "I wish Diarmad hadn't turned me down."

"Wait, someone turned you down?" she asked.

"Well, technically, he just accepted an alternate position and is the head of security for my castle," I explained.

"Oh, that guy. Yeah, it is a shame, but he's probably happier being away from your craziness and living a quiet life keeping paparazzi away from your castle." She smiled. "So, who are you thinking?"

"I think I'll reach out to the fighter and set up an interview with him," I said. "He's been working at one of our businesses as a bouncer, and despite it paying well, I don't think it's really taking all his skills into account."

"That's a perfect way to phrase the offer of the position," she said and patted my shoulder. "You're learning so fast! I'm so proud. I'll make a super mafia queen out of you soon."

CHAPTER THIRTEEN

The MMA fighter, Hal "Hunter" Harris, was younger than I expected, twenty-four years old, and had a quiet intensity that I liked.

"When do I start?" he asked after I offered the position.

"You don't even know what the pay is," I said softly.

He shifted on the chair to lean forward. "Mrs. Moriarty—"

"Amelia."

"Amelia, I know that being a bodyguard to the CEO of Moriarty Technology, also our boss's wife, will pay more than my bouncer job, so that's all I need to know."

"Hal—"

"Hunter," he said with a smirk.

"Hunter, you realize that you'll have to live here with us?" I asked.

"Amelia, we explained everything to him. He's not going into this blind, and he said he didn't have any questions," Forrest reminded me.

"I understand what my job is and accept it. I will protect you and your family at all times. I actually did a little bodyguard work for Mr. Gregori at a couple of meetings and events for his wife before I joined the Moriarty Mafia."

Erina had mentioned that to me.

"Well, if you understand and accept, let's move on to the awful part of this and have you fill out the paperwork." I smiled as I said it, and he returned the smile.

Once he'd signed everything, including the non-disclosure agreement, I stood and held out my hand to shake his.

"Welcome aboard!"

He shook my hand and nodded. "I can start as soon as I pick up my stuff from my apartment."

"Already handled," Dane said as he came into the living room. "Your things will be delivered to your room in an hour."

"Great," he said and turned to me. "What's on your agenda for the day?"

"We have work this morning, so we'll be heading into the office, and then this evening, we will be relaxing at home for once," I said.

"Actually," Dane said, "you and Arcadio have a date tonight, don't you?"

"Tomorrow," I amended. "Arcadio and I are going out tomorrow. We decided we wanted to do a daytime date instead of an evening date."

"For dates, do you want me to just secure the perimeter and keep away fans or paparazzi?" Hunter asked.

I hadn't thought about him coming with us during dates, but as my new bodyguard, he should go with me everywhere. "I guess."

"Just blend into the place they go to," Dane instructed. "You'll really just be backup in case anything happens that whoever she is out with can't handle."

Hunter nodded, his short, brown shaggy hair bouncing. "Understood."

"You sure we shouldn't test him first?" Arcadio asked from the doorway.

"You have seen his fights," I reminded him. "I don't think you need to test him."

"I think he just wants to spar," Dane said and looked at Hunter. "I can't say I don't feel the same."

I turned to Hunter. "It's up to you, but you don't have to spar with them. You've already got the job, no matter what they say."

He shrugged a shoulder. "Sparring is good; it keeps you limber and in shape. Plus, it's a great way to start the day."

"Well, then let's head down to the gym. We might as well give you a tour on the way." I walked out of the room, and the men followed behind me. Hunter, on my right, eyes scanning everything as we walked.

"The bedrooms are here," I said and indicated the doors we walked by. "The nursery is the middle door on the left. Paige and Callen go with us to the office now and go to the on-site daycare." We continued down the hallways, and I continued with the tour. The only reaction I got from him was once we reached the gym, and he saw inside.

"This is...amazing," he said as he looked at all the equipment.

"My men like to stay in shape so keep the best equipment here. We've even got some prototypes that haven't launched yet," I said, feeling smug, even though I hadn't picked the stuff out, just helped organize it a bit better.

The guys removed their shoes and jackets while I leaned against a wall.

"Don't break him," I called out.

"You talking to him or me?" Arcadio asked.

I winked and said nothing, which made Hunter laugh.

"No hitting in the face," Arcadio instructed. "We wouldn't want any bruising to show."

"Got it. Body shots all day," Hunter said with a smile.

Yeah, he was going to fit in well with everyone.

They put padded gloves on, the kind MMA fighters used that allowed them to still grapple, and bowed to each other.

"Remember! You're only sparring!" I shouted.

Arcadio and Hunter danced around each other, throwing a couple of jabs here and there, but looked like they were mainly testing each other out.

Suddenly, Arcadio darted forward, his fist connecting with Hunter's stomach.

Hunter didn't seem fazed, though; he just darted back and then right into Arcadio again and hit him in the stomach.

The two started moving faster and faster, and then, suddenly, Hunter was on his back, tapping the mat. "I yield."

Arcadio held out his hand and helped Hunter up. "You weren't trying your hardest, were you?"

Hunter stood and shrugged. "I haven't fought in months. I'm used to breaking up bar fights now."

"You'll definitely need that skill with Amelia to guard," Arcadio said.

"Hey!" I yelled and threw a towel at Arcadio.

He caught it and blew me a kiss.

"We better head out," Dane said. "As much as I'd love to go a round, we have work to get to."

"Shea is getting Paige and Callen ready," Forrest added. "He's probably waiting for one of us to give him a hand carrying them and the diaper bags."

"Do I need to wear anything specific?" Hunter asked.

"We'll get you a suit this weekend," Dane answered. "You'll just be with her in her office today, so no one will really notice."

Hunter nodded his understanding, and we all headed to the front.

I took Paige from Shea and cuddled her against my chest. "Hi, Paige-y Wagey. Mama missed you."

She babbled nonsense and cuddled against me.

Callen sniffled, and his eyes started to tear up. "Mama. Ma. Ma!"

"Someone's jealous," Shea chuckled and switched babies with me.

I kissed Callen's plump cheeks and rubbed my nose against his. "Spoiled boy, Mama loves you, too."

He opened his mouth and gave me a "kiss" on the cheek, pressing his open mouth to my face.

I kissed him back several times. "So cute. You're going to destroy some poor girl's heart; I just know it."

"Or several," Stephan said as he walked out of the house and kissed Callen's cheek and then mine. "If he's anything like me."

"I bet you destroyed hundreds of girls' hearts," I muttered. "Heartbreaker."

"No, that was Dane," he said and pointed his thumb over his shoulder.

"Hey! Don't get her started," Dane snapped.

Stephan shook Hunter's hand. "Nice to have you on board. Please, protect my wife."

Hunter nodded. "With my life, sir."

Stephan patted his upper back and then climbed into the car.

I handed Callen to Dane, who had climbed inside so he

could buckle Callen into the car seat.

"We have an interview today," Stephan informed me.

"What kind of interview?" I asked.

"Television," he replied and smiled wide.

I groaned and slid into my seat. "Wonderful."

"It will be your time to set the record straight," Stephan said. "Everyone loves you once they meet you, and the average citizen will be the same. You just have to explain that Shea was talking big like most men do when trying to impress the girl they like."

"What do I say about Holmes?"

"They won't ask," he said confidently. "They know that I'll destroy their company if they mention his name."

"What about—"

Stephan turned around and smiled. "Darling, you're going to be fine. If you're uncertain about answering a question, just squeeze my hand, and I'll help."

"You'll be sitting right beside me?" I asked.

He nodded. "Throughout the entire interview."

"Is this a live studio audience interview?" Hunter asked.

Stephan looked up and smiled. "Excellent question. Yes, it is."

"I'll be there as Stephan's guard," Shea informed Hunter. "So, you'll be my backup, and your primary objective will be to protect Amelia, should shit hit the fan."

"As things tend to do when Amelia is involved," Stephan said and winked at me.

"Rude!" I yelled, folded my arms across my chest, and slumped back in my seat. Rude, but true, so I wouldn't say more.

My husbands all laughed.

"I demand sushi for lunch as recompense," I said sternly.

"Oh, she's definitely learning from Erina," Dane commented.

"No, that sounded more like Marlee," Shea countered.

"Yeah," Stephan agreed. "That's definitely more Marlee."

"I'm so telling them you said that." I shook my head and pulled out my phone to see a message from my mom telling me to keep a smile on during my interview and that Randolph was handling as much as he could on the internet.

I set my phone down and looked at Stephan. He'd turned to face forward in his seat and was chatting with Forrest about something as Shea drove.

"Stephan, did you hire Randolph?"

Everyone turned to look at me; even Shea looked up at the rearview mirror to look at me.

"Perhaps," he said. "Is that a problem?"

"Who is Randolph?" Hunter asked Arcadio, who sat beside him.

"One of her mother's husbands," Arcadio answered.

"Perhaps means Randolph started doing things, and you hired him to keep you apprised," I said. "Right?"

Stephan's eyes widened, and then he cocked his head slightly as he looked at me. "You've become very observant and learned about me quickly. It's…a little disconcerting."

"I also know Randolph and know that as soon as articles went up on the internet mentioning me, he was likely all over it."

"We're tracking where the articles and photos are coming from," Stephan explained. "We have a feeling that these have not been coincidences."

I nodded. "Erina felt the same."

He scowled. "She did?"

I nodded. "Mr. Collman was meeting with Connor when I was there for my girls' day."

Stephan looked ready to murder someone. "Why didn't you tell me about this?" He looked back at Forrest. "Why wasn't I apprised?"

"Nothing happened," Forrest said. "I thought you would have already known. Sorry, boss."

"Forrest pulled his gun on him," I added with a smirk.

Forrest shot me an annoyed glare before looking back at Stephan. "He appeared behind us, and I reacted. Gregori and his men weren't upset."

"They actually complimented him on his fast draw," I said.

Stephan ran a hand down his face. "Dammit, what is that bastard up to? He doesn't have a sick friend here that we could find, but I also haven't found anything suggesting he is up to something."

"Sowing seeds of discord," Hunter said.

We all looked at him.

He fidgeted a second and then tensed and straightened. "A man who has nothing to lose but everything to gain could possibly be here just to sow seeds of discord around you and your company."

"Has he requested a meeting?" I asked Stephan.

Stephan shook his head.

"Well, let's just keep an eye on him. I don't need to add anything else to my plate today since you're already forcing me to go do this interview."

———

"Mrs. Moriarty, is it true that your conversation was taken out of context? That the video clip doesn't tell the full story?"

Wendy, the beautiful talk show host with cleavage spilling out the top of her dress, asked.

"It was taken completely out of context," I said with a nod. "Shea was simply doing what men do, telling you that he'd protect you no matter what."

"And the 'murder hobo' comment? What was that in reference to?" she asked.

"Wendy, have you ever heard of Dungeons & Dragons? It's a roleplaying game we play, and in it, a lot of times, you end up having to kill a bunch of people. There's a term the community uses for those of us who end up with a 'kill now, worry about it later' mentality, and that's where we got murder hobo from. It's not real; it's just all fake, role-playing. I'm not really killing dragons either, but my character does in the game."

Several of the audience had cheered when I mentioned the game, and several laughed and clapped when I finished talking.

"You know, it's just really frustrating to be villainized like this when I'm just trying to figure out my place and accept this crazy reality that is my life." I looked over at Stephan with a loving smile, pulled our joined hands up so I could kiss his hand, and said, "I mean, I never ever thought I'd be able to say that I married this amazing man."

The crowd whistled and cheered.

"I am the lucky one in this relationship," Stephan said, leaned over, and kissed my cheek.

The crowd exploded in "aw"s.

"Could you explain to us how your relationship works? From what we've seen, she's not only with you but also with your guard and right-hand men. Is that true?"

Stephan nodded. "We all love Amelia and are completely

devoted to her. She's an incredibly special woman, and the five of us were surprised and ecstatic when we found someone who fit our group so well."

"So, she is in a relationship with all of you, but you all don't have other relationships?" Wendy asked.

"Correct," Stephan said. He smiled adoringly at me and said, "She's more than enough woman for all of us. She loves us all too equally to choose between us. Instead of risking losing her, or our friendships, we accepted each of us will always have a special place in her heart."

There were a few whistles and catcalls, but I didn't mind.

"Does that mean that you...share her?" Wendy asked.

I looked at her and said, "Wendy, this is a daytime show! I don't think that answer would be appropriate for some of your younger audiences." I winked.

She fanned her face. "Well, I think that answers well enough. I'm curious, though, do you not think it's unfair for her to have multiple lovers while you all share one?"

"None of us is here against our will," Stephan said. "We love Amelia. There is no other woman for us and never will be. We know that most of the world won't understand, but this is how we wish to live our lives, and if we aren't hurting anyone else, then why does it matter? My poor wife has been villainized for doing nothing more than loving her husbands and taking on her role as my wife very seriously. She actually designed a new technology that will revolutionize the fashion industry."

"Oh?" Wendy asked, her eyes wide. "You don't happen to have a sneak peek for us, do you?"

"I do, actually," Stephan said.

Now my eyes were wide. I hadn't known he was going to reveal the mirror to the public during this.

Some of the crew rolled out one of the mirrors and turned it to face the audience.

"That's a lovely mirror," Wendy commented.

"Oh, it's not *just* a mirror," Stephan said. He looked at me. "Why don't you explain what it does while I show them."

"This mirror allows you to see what you would look like in an outfit without actually having to change into it," I explained.

Stephan stood in front of the mirror, scrolled over to the winter collection, and chose a skiing outfit.

The crowd gasped.

"As you can see, it shows Stephan what he would look like in that outfit. You input your measurements, and it will even tell you what size to purchase for that look."

"That's amazing!" Wendy praised, and several people clapped.

"I know many, like me, don't enjoy the shopping process, and some just don't want to be out around so many people at once. This mirror allows you to bypass that, or at least virtually try on some outfits before going to the store, so you only have to try on a couple instead of a dozen."

Stephan switched to the swimsuit catalog, and I bit my lip to hide my smile as his reflection showed him shirtless and in a pair of boardshorts.

The crowd whistled and cheered.

"If you take pictures in your underwear, it can even show you outfits like this," I explained. "This is hooked up to the online stores, but the camera is not accessible by outsiders, so you don't need to worry about anyone gaining access to the images."

"My team has ensured the security measures are top-notch," Stephan said as he walked to my side, put his arm around my waist, and pulled me against his side. "Isn't she amazing? Can you not see why I love her?"

I raised up on my toes and kissed him lightly on the lips. "I love you more and more every day."

He rubbed the ends of our noses together, and the audience went crazy.

"That's all for today's episode!" Wendy announced. "Check out the new invention by Mrs. Moriarty at Moriarty Technology today. Thank you, Mr. and Mrs. Moriarty, for visiting us today. We hope your love continues to bloom."

Stephan and I lifted our hands in a wave while smiling wide.

As soon as we were off-air, I threw my arms around Stephan's neck and hugged him. "Thank you."

He squeezed me and kissed the side of my head. "You're welcome, darling."

"Here's some water," Hunter said and held out a bottle to me.

"Thank you." I drank some and then handed the bottle to Stephan as we headed into the back to go home.

"Great job," Shea praised. "You two did amazing."

"I can't believe you brought the mirror," I said and looked over at Stephan.

"It was the perfect opportunity to showcase your invention. Plus, Wendy will take our side in most future events now that we've given her show a significant ratings boost," he explained.

His phone dinged with a message, and he smiled as he read it. "You've already hit one hundred pre-orders."

I stopped walking, mouth open, and stared at him. "You're serious?"

He nodded and showed me the message from our marketing department.

"That's crazy!" I squealed.

"Let's celebrate," Stephan said. "I owe you sushi anyway, so let's go now."

"Sushi places won't open for an hour," I reminded him.

He gave me a look.

Oh, right. Billionaire.

"Suggestion," Shea said.

"Let's ask Sasuke to come to the house and invite Erina and Marlee over to celebrate as well. They did help you a lot with this, and it was Erina who mentioned the app idea that sparked all of this."

"That's a great idea!" I said to Shea. "You're so smart."

"I'm not just brawn, but brains, too," he said and winked as he flexed one arm in his button-up shirt.

"Don't flex too much, or you'll tear it," I teased.

"You wish," he scoffed.

I sent a message to Erina and Marlee, inviting them over, and then skipped out ahead of the guys. "Today's been great so far."

"I've got to get back to the office so I can shoot the commercial," Stephan commented as he looked at his phone.

"Commercial for what?" I asked.

He winked. "A secret."

"I'll just hack your calendar," I murmured.

Shea smacked my butt. "No. Bad wife." Shea's phone rang, and he answered immediately. "Sup?"

"Such a professional answer," I teased.

Shea rolled his eyes but scowled when the person on the phone said something. "No, just keep them at the front. We're on our way back."

He locked his phone, and we all looked at him expectantly as we stood in the elevator.

"Angel Eyes is in the lobby, asking to meet with you."

"Really?" Stephan asked.

"Not you, boss. Amelia," Shea explained.

Stephan scowled. "Does he want me to kill him? Is he trying to piss me off enough to the point that I make him disappear?"

I set my hand on his arm. "Deep breath, Stephan. He's just pulling your chain, but don't let him get to you." I smirked. "Let him meet with me. We've got surveillance up, and I've got a new guard. Plus, you know I'm packing."

Hunter looked at me with wide eyes. "You are?"

I nodded. "Always."

"She got abducted once before, and since then, we've made her keep weapons on her at all times," Shea explained.

"She's a danger magnet," Stephan added with a smile.

I mocked him. "And you're all rude."

"Oh, there's an article already up with clips from Wendy's show," Shea said.

I looked over at his phone and was glad to finally see a positive article about me. "Finally, some good publicity."

"I added a bonus to your pay this month," Stephan informed me. "It's for your invention."

My mouth dropped. "What? You're not supposed to give *me* bonuses."

"Why not?" he asked. "I give the others bonuses."

"My team—"

"They all got bonuses, too," Stephan said. "You guys earned it for all your hard work."

I pulled up my banking information and blinked. "What

the hell, Stephan? That's too much." I felt like I was going to faint.

Hunter put a hand on my lower back to keep me steady. "Big, deep breaths."

"That's just the beginning. When sales start going through, you'll get a percentage of that as well," Stephan said.

I had so much money that I didn't even know what to do with it.

"Oh, and I have one more surprise for you, but you'll have to wait to get it until tonight." He winked at me, knowing I hated surprises.

"You're cruel!" I accused and hissed at him.

"Did she just hiss at him?" Hunter asked.

"Yep," Shea said, "you get used to it."

"I'll meet with Angel Eyes. I don't want you anywhere near him," Stephan said and kissed my head as he and Shea left.

CHAPTER FOURTEEN

"Congratulations, Amelia!" everyone cheered and clinked their glasses together. The living room was decorated with streamers and balloons, which made me smile.

The internet had blown up; social media shares of the clips of Stephan in the boardshorts had skyrocketed my invention's premiere, and I had thousands of pre-orders now.

"I knew you could make something epic," Erina praised and hugged me, squishing our cheeks together as she did. "You're amazing."

"It's all thanks to you," I said and squeezed her back. "Thank you for always encouraging me."

"Hey! I encouraged you, too!" Marlee said as she stomped over and squished us both in a tight hug.

We chuckled as we hugged, and I felt like I might cry. Having such supportive friends in my corner was the best.

"In celebration of her success, I have two gifts," Stephan said.

"Two?" I gasped.

He picked up a TV remote, turned on the television, and

then hit play. I stared in shock, excitement, and laughter that turned into tears of joy as my husbands all appeared in an advertisement for my mirror, showing off their muscular bodies while using the mirror to try on various outfits.

They'd also gotten a few female models, but my husbands were the main attraction. The part that likely had all these women pre-ordering was the free calendar featuring my husbands that came with every pre-order.

"What marketing genius came up with that idea?" I asked as I wiped at my cheeks.

Marlee raised her hand. "I suggested it as a joke, not thinking they'd actually go through with it."

"How could we not?" Dane asked with a smile. "We knew it would make Amelia smile."

"I love you guys," I sniffled.

"One more gift," Stephan said. "It's outside, though."

"Outside?" I asked as he took my hand and led me out to the front door and to the driveway.

In front of the house sat the beautiful dark blue sports car I'd had my eye on with a big red bow tied to the roof.

My mouth opened and closed a few times, like a fish out of water, but no sound came out. I approached the car slowly, like it might disappear, and tentatively set my hand on the hood.

"It's mine? Just mine?" I asked.

Stephan set the keys in my hand. "It's all yours."

I squealed, hugged him, and then slid into the driver's seat, stroking the steering wheel.

My own car.

Stephan slid into the passenger seat and asked, "What are you waiting for? Let's take it out for a test drive."

"Is...is that okay?" I asked. It was a two-seater, so no one else could join us. We would be alone, without bodyguards.

"Who runs this business?" he asked and arched a brow.

"You," I answered with a smile and pushed down the button to start the car.

He set his hand on mine when it came to rest on the shifter. "Us," he corrected. "You and I run the business."

"Are you saying you're going to let me be more involved in the mafia side?" I asked softly.

He nodded. "It's time that I fully let you in on everything. You're my partner, and it's only fair that you know everything. At this point, the feds wouldn't care if you were oblivious; they'd still try to give you jail time."

I kissed him and smiled so wide I felt like my face might split. "I love you."

"I love you, too," he said and smiled wide. "Now, let's go for a drive."

I peeled out of the driveway and out onto the street. Thankfully, no one used the road since it just led to our house, so I didn't have to worry about the possibility of other cars.

"Oh, one other thing," Stephan said when I made a U-turn to head back home.

"Another thing?" I asked.

"Erina will explain when we get home."

I floored it to get home as fast as possible, which made Stephan laugh.

After jerking the e-brake up, I stumbled out of the car and ran to Erina. "What?" I panted.

My husbands all shook their heads at me but were smiling wide.

She put her hand on her stomach and smiled. "I'm pregnant."

Marlee and I screamed, hugged Erina, and then danced around her.

"Yes!" we yelled.

"I get to be an auntie!" I yelled and then leaned over to kiss her cheek.

"Yes, you do," she agreed.

My life had fallen apart for a bit but seemed to be bouncing back even better.

Erina wiped my face. "Why are you crying? I'm the hormonal one."

"Everything got all crazy and messed up, but now things are even better than before," I sniffled.

"Give it time," Dane said. "Craziness will come back again."

"Speaking of craziness, we've got some big plans next weekend. Erina, I'll need your help," Forrest said.

Erina's eyes widened. "My help?"

"And Marlee's," Forrest said.

I narrowed my eyes. "Excuse me?"

He winked. "Don't worry about it, babe. Just know that you'll enjoy the surprise we are concocting."

"I hate surprises. You do this on purpose, don't you? You could have messaged them separately without talking in front of me."

"Where's the fun in that?" he asked as he kissed my cheek.

"So, who's ready for sushi?" Stephan asked and clapped his hands together.

"Me!" I yelled and linked arms with Erina as we headed back inside the house.

"I'll stick to the cooked rolls," she said with a chuckle.

"Oh, no!" I gasped and stopped walking. "You can't drink anymore."

"It's a travesty!" Marlee gasped and put her hand to her

head like she might faint. Brian fanned her face, encouraging her display.

"I'll just drink virgin drinks," Erina said. "No biggie. We endured it for Amelia, so I know you two will endure it for me, too."

"Of course we will," I said with a firm nod.

"We get to plan a baby shower!" Marlee exclaimed.

"Yes!" I exclaimed back. "It's going to be the best baby shower ever!"

"It's going to be insanity," Erina muttered.

"You'll love it, don't fret," I assured her.

Stephan chatted with everyone as we ate sushi the chef prepared and drank delicious drinks.

"So, are you excited for your next interview now that the first is out of the way?" Marlee asked me.

I scoffed and shook my head. "Not by a long shot. I wish that I didn't have to do anymore."

"Actually," Stephan said, "we don't have to do anymore. That one was enough."

I pretended like I was going to faint, and Hunter pushed me back up. "Serious?"

He nodded. "Yep. You made such a great impression that clips have been shared much more than anticipated, so we don't need to do more interviews to clear us. You've become America's Darling in a single afternoon."

"Fuck yeah!" I screamed and fist-pumped the air.

That made everyone laugh.

I stood off to the side to enjoy watching my friends and family. All of the insanity I had had to endure was definitely worth it in the end when I got to enjoy things like this. When I could enjoy my favorite people all in one room, talking and laughing.

My life wasn't perfect, but it was pretty damn close.

"Oh, we just received word," Forrest said. "Angel Eyes left the state, took a plane, and returned home."

I looked over at Stephan. "Did you meet with him? What did he want?"

Stephan's face darkened, and he said, "I told him if he wanted to live, he had better leave my territory in the next three hours."

My brows flew up into my hairline. "Why did you threaten him? What did he ask for?"

Stephan looked over at me, and there was a ferocity about him that he usually hid. "He wanted you. Offered me one billion dollars for you."

My jaw dropped. "He…he offered to *buy* me?"

Stephan stalked over to me and gripped my upper arms gently. "I turned him down without hesitation."

"One billion dollars," I whispered. "Wow."

"Rude!" Erina said. "Connor was only offered one *million* dollars for me."

"Let's just hope he got the message and stays out of my territory," Stephan said. "If he crosses again, I'll kill him. I won't let him touch you."

I kissed his cheek and smiled. "Don't worry, I'm sure we won't see him again."

Knowing my luck, though, we'd probably see him much sooner than expected.

CONTINUE THE SERIES...

If you enjoyed SUDDENLY BARONESS, check out the next book in the series...**UNEXPECTED ASSASSINS**

http://catbanks.co/AMS

CONNECT WITH CATHERINE BANKS

I really appreciate you reading my book! I hope you enjoyed it.

Please consider leaving a review at your favorite site.

Here are some ways to connect with me:

Check out my Website:

www.catherinebanks.com

Follow me on BookBub:

https://www.bookbub.com/authors/catherine-banks

Join my Patreon:

http://www.patreon.com/catherinebanks

Purchase items handmade by Catherine:

http://Etsy.com/shop/TurboKittenInd

ABOUT THE AUTHOR

Catherine Banks is a USA Today bestselling fantasy author who writes in several fantasy subgenres and has multiple pseudonyms. She began writing fiction at only four years old and finished her first full-length novel at the age of fifteen. She is married to her soulmate and best friend, Avery, who she has two amazing children with. After her full-time job, she reads books, plays video games, and watches anime shows and movies with her family to relax. Although she has lived in Northern California her entire life, she dreams of traveling around the world. Catherine is also C.E.O. of Turbo Kitten Industries™, a company with many hats including being a book publisher and Etsy store full of nerdy fun.

facebook.com/catherinebanksauthor
twitter.com/catherineebanks
amazon.com/author/catherinebanks
bookbub.com/authors/catherine-banks

MORE FROM CATHERINE BANKS

YOUNG ADULT PARANORMAL & FANTASY ROMANCE SERIES

Artemis Lupine Series
Song of the Moon
Kiss of a Star
Healed by the Fire
Battles of the Night
Artemis Lupine, The Complete Series

Little Death Bringer Duology
Mercenary
Protector
Little Death Bringer, The Official Coloring Book

Pirate Princess Series
Pirate Princess
Princess Triumvirate

ADULT PARANORMAL & FANTASY ROMANCE SERIES
Zodiac Shifters Paranormal Romance Series
Centaur's Prize

Tiger Tears

Lion About

Ciara Steele Novella Series
True Faces

Barbaric Tendencies

ADULT REVERSE HAREM PARANORMAL & FANTASY ROMANCE SERIES
Her Royal Harem Series
Royally Entangled

Royally Exposed

Royally Elected

Royally Enraged

Her Royal Harem, The Complete Series

The Demon's Fair

Her Royal Harem, The Coloring Book

Wings of Vengeance Series
Of Dragons and Cruelty

Of Minotaurs and Sacrifice

Wings of Vengeance, The Complete Series

Anderelle: Minloa Trilogy
Queen of the Stars

Empress of the Galaxy

Goddess of the Universe

Anderelle: Minloa, The Complete Series

Bonds of Madness Series
Sealing the Deal
Racing the Clock

Her Super Harem Series
Lucky Strike

Her Hellish Harem Duet
A Demon's Heart
A Demon's Soul*

VELLA ADULT PARANORMAL REVERSE HAREM ROMANCE
Shark (Season One)

*Coming Soon

MORE FROM CATHERINE BANKS

STANDALONE YOUNG ADULT PARANORMAL &
FANTASY ROMANCE BOOKS
Monster Academy
Daughter of Lions
Lady Serra and the Draconian
Of Sky and Sea
The Last Werewolf
Sybil Deceived
An Outcast Among Wolves

STANDALONE YOUNG ADULT PARANORMAL &
FANTASY REVERSE HAREM ROMANCE BOOKS
Moon Academy

STANDALONE ADULT PARANORMAL & FANTASY ROMANCE BOOKS

Demonic Contract

Anja's Secret

Dragon's Blood

Last Ama Princess

Transforming Rose

Alys of Asgard

Phoenix Possessed

Stone Heart

STANDALONE URBAN FANTASY BOOKS

The Pawn

CHILDREN'S BOOKS

Calvin's Alien Adventure

MORE FROM DAISY EMORY

The Boyfriend Deal

Their Purple Girl

Courting Love

*Coming Soon